# ROBOWOK

## BY
## AXEL T. HARPER

Translated from
Dutch by Ciarán Ó Faoláin

Ballast Books, LLC
www.ballastbooks.com



ISBN: 978-1-964934-11-2 (paperback)
ISBN: 978-1-964934-25-9 (ebook)

Printed in the United States of America

Published by Ballast Books
www.ballastbooks.com

For more information, bulk orders, appearances,
or speaking requests,
please email: info@ballastbooks.com

# CONTENTS

# 1. DAVID

So there he is, sitting in his private hammam. Through the thick man-made fog, David sees his insignia on the glass door. The architect had convinced him that having his own insignia throughout his entire home would give it that extra touch of class—that it would, as he put it, transform it into a résidence. He'd roll the R and draw out the nasal *-ence* before pronouncing the final E: "*résiden-n-n-nsuh*." And when you said "résidence" that way, you just had to add a lot more gestural flourishes and nasally inflected grimacing than one could ever hope to see accompanying the little pedestrian word "house." The main reason David had agreed to the insignia, in fact, was to get past all this high theatricality. Good architects were hard to come by these days.

The hammam was made for eight adults. David sat there on his own. It was Tuesday afternoon. He hadn't been awake that long.

Around eleven o'clock that morning, he'd started with a hand-pressed newspaper. He'd always skip quickly past the domestic news stories, past the politics and society pages, to sports and economics—the only things that mattered in the world as far as he was concerned. He was looking above all for stories about start-ups or young sports talents who were nurturing big dreams.

This morning's stories were mostly about clumsy big businesses run by what he saw as even clumsier bosses, who had what they called "plans for innovation." "We're going to be doing things radically differently," they'd say, and then reel off a slew of buzzwords such as "the cloud," "mobile," and "holacracy." Not even a quarter of the way through that story, David had given up.

The kitchen had clearly done its best with his breakfast. He'd already fallen out with them over the thickness of the yogurt and how much milk they'd put in his cappuccino.

David hadn't been born a nasty or an especially spoiled person; he'd been forced to become one—or rather, he acted that way for the sake of his staff. At least that was how he saw it.

After finishing with the newspaper, he'd turned to the day ahead. A businessman from up north might be coming to pitch his invention, and in the evening, he'd been invited to a fair for those willing to pay an entrance fee of "just" 2,000 euros. David had decided then and there not to go.

To give a bit of purpose to his life, he'd decided to go do some sports. He'd called his personal trainer over, only to end up doing exercises for way too much per hour while someone barked in his ear. The barking had gone on and on and on, so it no longer had any effect; at a certain point, he was going through the motions not because he was being barked at but just so he could say he'd done what he'd set out to do.

He was not unhappy after he'd finished. After his allegedly super healthy shake, which he'd had mainly to keep the kitchen busy, he'd earned the trip to his hammam.

And that was where he was now, looking at a fogged-over door with a specially designed insignia sporting his initials—and a bear. The architect considered lions, elephants, tigers, and birds to be too clichéd, but he'd never seen a bear at any of his clients' houses, even though it had much more of an *aura* about it. Well that's what he said. It was clear he didn't know any financial market lingo.

David had been staring blankly in front of him in the hammam for so long that the skin on his fingertips looked like a forty-year-old version of himself. He stood up, stretched, and walked to his ice-cold shower.

When it came time for the ice-cold shower, David wasn't allowed to be a wuss; the plaster had to be snatched off in one go. His body was shocked by the freezing water that pummeled him thick and fast—but his expression didn't change. He just stared out in front of him, counting down in his head from twenty to zero.

His bathrobe—also emblazoned with his insignia—was hanging there, waiting for him.

He skipped lunch, just as he had done in the past. "In the past" made it sound like it had been ages, but how long ago could it really have been? After all, he'd been just twenty-seven when he sold his company

In any case, it felt like a completely different life. He'd get up early, while the world still slept, and then have a coffee for breakfast. He'd have his phone in one hand showing the latest figures and would put on his clothes with the other, like a seasoned contortionist, as he headed toward the door.

Lunch was a purely professional affair—a check to make sure the machines were working properly that day and that the ingredients were as fresh as all the messages promised. The joy of lunch had long since disappeared.

All these years, he had been eating the same limited variations several times a day. Rice or noodles. With chicken, beef, shrimp, and/or veggies. And finally, orange, hoisin, black bean, or green sauce. To consumers, it seemed like so many degrees of freedom. For David, the range of options was more like a weather forecast in the north of Scotland: cats and dogs or rain just bucketing down.

Now David could have any lunch he wanted. In the beginning, he'd taken full advantage of that. But then that freedom too had turned out to be worth less than it'd been cracked up to be. Often, it was an Italian roll with cheese, ham, or both. Or like today, having lunch would've felt like overdoing it.

David had so much time on his hands. He had looked forward to that time as much as he had to the options for lunch. He had daydreamed about the possibilities: traveling, watching films, playing sports, just hanging out with friends. He wandered around in the western part of the front of the house. In his head there was a long list of possibilities, but the rest of his body did not feel any sensation at all in response to any of them.

The men in the garden were busy, and if the green mountain that stood among them was anything to go by, they must have started early. David did everything he could to avoid being seen. There was an enormous risk that he'd be forced into some chit-chat.

Like a spy in a movie, he moved as stealthily and invisibly as he could from one side of the room to the other. He managed it. But once he'd arrived safely, there wasn't much to do on this side of the room either. This was not because of the options before him, all of which were within easy reach: a pool table, stacks of books, old-fashioned stacks of DVDs (all box sets he could not have afforded before the streaming era), and an unpacked consumer electronics item that had seemed to promise, when he'd bought it, to make his life better. David was like the ten-year-old son of a billionaire—though he had all the playthings in the world, he still had nothing to play with.

The truth was that he just had to start over, to start building again—to do what he had been born to do. This had already been the conclusion several times based on several expensive sessions with people who had studied the issue he was having. Each time, the diplomas on the wall had given David confidence that this person with such-and-such a title was going to help him find himself again—a new purpose in his life.

And each time, these learned individuals had helped him to reach the same understanding, the same insights, which were nothing if not crashingly obvious.

There had already been ideas. He'd even bought a domain name for a six-figure sum from an American in the midwestern United States. However, despite the investments made in them, all the ideas had died a death for want of any relevance to the world. If they couldn't exercise any fascination over him after three weeks, how could he possibly spend years on them?

So there he was, waiting for inspiration. He'd even tried to force things by going on a number of inspirational trips and speaking to several "innovators." And it had all been rather underwhelming. The "innovations" were often variations on the same themes, based on the same trends, applications of the same old new technologies.

A few weeks earlier, it had gotten to the point where he'd ordered an old-fashioned multi-volume encyclopedia. After delivery, he had put them all in a catapult he had jerry-rigged. After firing it, he'd grabbed the farthest book, closed his eyes, opened the book blindly at a random page, and put his finger on it.

His hope was that the word his finger landed on would give him the inspiration he was so desperate for. The project, which lasted days, had given him words and names such as stratigraphy, sholes, Elbrus, nettle, and hit parade. He'd then spent a lot of time trying to explain to himself what might have given him the idea that this brainwave could ever have worked.

And then there was the acceptance phase. Perhaps he was allowed just the one truly disruptive idea. And like everyone else, he had to go and call something ordinary "disruptive" when those in the know would realize it was just a logical variation on an already existing consumer proposition. Perhaps he'd even have to stoop to doing a business-to-business proposition or, worse yet, make himself useful as a consultant, sharing his knowledge and skills with large companies that were desperate to produce any kind of innovation or change.

There were times when David was about to go that route. Money was no longer an issue; he was no longer laboring under the illusion that there would be a form of consumption that could give him meaning.

Creation—that was the answer. Leaving something behind—a legacy. Recently, he'd devoted himself entirely to his house, his very own Hearst Castle, complete with the obligatory insignia. He would bequeath to humankind something tangible: a daring edifice that would be celebrated for generations for its progressiveness, ingenuity, and general benevolence to humankind.

The design phase had given him some false hope. Nothing was too over the top for the architect. And the many technical people who had been brought in had presented him with a slew of state-of-the-art technologies that they said would make his house more cutting edge than anything in the places you'd expect to find "cutting edge," like Silicon Valley.

But then city officials came onto the scene, and that was when the fun quickly stopped. Trying to make the building regulations and the aesthetic conditions work together seemed for a while to be an interesting puzzle, but it soon turned out to be a merciless killer of any kind of creativity.

By contrast with his business ideas, in this case, David did feel some kind of pressure to complete the project. The last few months had been an internal struggle. How was it that someone with so much money and so much time on their hands could do such mind-numbing things, all of which manifested themselves in such utter mediocrity?

To amuse himself, David liked to look for boundaries and see how far he could go in terms of size, height, and execution without the officials being able to nix the project with their rules. It had all resulted in a gigantic building with an elevator that went from two floors below ground to five floors above ground and corridors to several elevators across the breadth of the house so one didn't have to go to a central point each time to go up or down.

He'd had an outdoor swimming pool dug but also a swimming pond, purely because the law allowed both. Both were as big as was legally allowed. There was also an indoor swimming pool, from which his private bowling alley could be seen through a giant glass wall. He knew less than nothing about bowling, but at a certain point, the logical uses for spaces had run out. *A bowling alley,* he'd thought, *might be fun for a party one day or could be a nice little feature when it came time to sell to another, much more eccentric billionaire at some point down the road.*

Throwing parties had never really been his thing. It wasn't that he was socially inept; as a teenager, he'd thrown plenty of parties. They just weren't fun for him anymore. A few months earlier, after the house had been finished, he'd thought briefly of planning a party—something after his druthers that would fascinate him and give someone else a new take on what parties could be. The inspiration didn't come in that case either, though, and the whole idea began to motivate him less and less.

# 2. BERNARD

"Fortunately, I was able to move some things around."

In recent years, Bernard had become a master at deluding himself—and others while he was at it—about how busy he was.

His online profile stated that he was active on several committees, associations, and commissions, but usually the companies or entities the profile referred to were hard to find online. Bernard was once asked about this and answered that these organizations would rather not garner any more attention than they were already getting.

"Tell me, which media house are you from, and in which titles are you planning to place this article about me?"

"Sorry, sir?" The journalist looked up as she rummaged in her backpack for paper, a pen, and a tripod for her iPhone.

"I'd understood from your correspondence that you have an international reach and that your main focus is on entrepreneurship. Do you write for the *Financial Times* or for the *Wall Street Journal* perhaps? I've been subscribing to both for years."

"Oh, um . . . I don't know either channel."

"Newspapers. Or in our new world do you call these titles 'channels'?"

"Ah, I see. Sorry for the confusion, sir. I do use pen and paper for small blog posts, but I don't write for a newspaper. I have a YouTube channel, and as of yesterday, as it happens, I have twenty thousand followers in over thirty countries."

Bernard found it difficult not to show his disappointment. He had told many of his friends several times the week before that a profile of him would be appearing in an internationally respected magazine or newspaper. He thought it was about time people read about his life and current views.

It was clear to him that the interview would mainly be about his son. However, he would certainly take the opportunity to talk about his own accomplishments whenever possible. What he himself had achieved was certainly nothing to sneeze at.

"I'll just adjust the lights if you don't mind, and then we can start."

"No problem, young lady. Is makeup still needed? Are you satisfied with my attire for this portrait?

The journalist was able to hold back her laughter just in time. Her sense of empathy was mature enough for her to see right away that the person she was pointing her phone at regarded himself as more than your average somebody.

"Where would you like to start? Perhaps I can begin by talking about my early childhood. I think—no, I know—that it had a considerable influence on who I would later become."

The journalist looked at her watch as inconspicuously as possible. She'd booked two hours for the interview. She'd already thought beforehand that this was far too much for the ten-minute clip she wanted to make. At this rate, though, it wasn't even clear whether she could make the date she'd planned for right after the interview. From the chats they'd had over the past few weeks, the guy she'd found on Tinder seemed promising.

"I was the youngest of five siblings and the only boy. And although I was the youngest, I soon turned out to be the leader of the five. That was no doubt because of my gender."

This remark was meant to be funny, but it kind of fell flat. The journalist couldn't manage a smile and didn't offer any confirmation of Bernard's hypothesis.

"My parents were poor—ours was a simple existence—but fortunately they had the wisdom and the foresight to prepare me for a better life. I was dressed in proper made-to-measure wear from an early age, and my mother spent a lot of time on our appearances and our language skills and made sure that we were in contact with their better clients from an early age."

"Clients?" The journalist surprised herself with her question, which popped out from genuine interest.

"My parents had a community establishment. One could have one's hair done there, among other things."

"A hair salon?"

Bernard took on a look that was both stern and disapproving and followed that up with a slight groan that said, *I've never been so insulted.*

"Apologies—a place for the community, you said?" The journalist had traveled an hour and a half to get here and didn't want to spoil things.

"Anyone who was anyone in our community would come by to talk about important issues in the current affairs of our great country and to represent both their own business interests and those of their clientele."

"I see." At that point, the journalist decided to leave the talking to Bernard so long as time allowed.

"At school, I stood head and shoulders above the other pupils. I invariably got good grades in all the subjects that mattered. Of course, I could have gone to one of the feeder schools for the better universities, but that was not in line with my ambitions, and my language skills were already at a level that would have prepared me for suitable roles. I was also a reasonably good sportsman. Unfortunately, though, my build was not quite according to the book. Otherwise I could have earned a good living for many years in any one of the many sports I was adept at.

I was always praised for my selflessness. From an early age, I let my deeds speak for themselves. I have always left it to others to promote me and themselves."

"And then you went to study?"

"I hadn't gotten up to that yet."

The journalist felt the watch on her wrist as if it were getting hotter and hotter. It was telling her what she already knew—that this was going to be a long day.

"Partly thanks to my mother, rest her soul, I learned at an early age that merely doing well at school and at the required extracurricular activities would not cut it."

"Cut it for what?"

Bernard had the immediate urge to snap back, "For what, *sir*?" But he realized that he was being filmed by the girl's phone and wanted to come across as a kindly man in his article.

"I have always had great ambitions. Many of my so-called peers simply wanted to go into business or become pastors, and some thought for a time that they could become professional sportsmen. However, I had a lot of plans. For example, I once gave a talk called 'A Day in the Life of the Prime Minister.' This was also meant to be preparatory work."

"Oh, I see. So you had political ambitions?"

"Fortunately, I found out in time that there is no money to be made there." Bernard blurted out a quick, arrogant laugh. "I learned from a classmate's brother that you have to be where the money is."

"Oil?"

"Ha! No. I mean banks, of course. That's where the money actually is."

"Of course. I could have thought of that myself."

"Indeed," he said, rather too curtly. He quickly realized that this did not make him seem like a likable character, even on film, so he added: "My brain, too, sometimes needs a little more time." *This remark more than makes up for the earlier one*, he thought.

"So you went to study business administration?"

"Ha! That course didn't exist back then, young lady. I became an economist. You have to nourish your brain with only the best."

"OK. So you were saying . . ."

"Yes. I could have gone anywhere, but of course I chose the oldest university with the best professors. Just diving into the books was not enough, of course, so right from the get-go, I spent more than half of my time on extracurricular activities. Such as . . ." Bernard made a drinking motion with his right hand and winked coyly at the journalist.

"And then you became a father?"

"We can talk about David in good time," Bernard responded irritably.

"Apologies. So you went to work?"

"Right. I had many choices after my studies, of course."

"Of course." The journalist barely managed to keep her remark free of sarcasm.

"But it was clear to anyone who knew anything about the world: I had to go to London. Top tier."

"Top tier?"

"Tier one. That's where it happens. Tier two and below—that's not real banking."

"Ah, I see." The journalist could not under-stand why she'd even thought to ask what "top tier" was.

"Those were crazy years. And I was at the top of my game."

"Oh—so you *did* actually become a top athlete after all!"

"Ha ha! Good one!"

Without even trying, the journalist had managed to charm Bernard. Perhaps that pro-duced some nice one-liners.

"Today, people whine that they are so busy. I used to work seven days a week. I ate, slept, and dreamt banking. *It* did not stop, so neither did I. But still—work hard, play hard, as they say."

"So you also made time to get up to some fun."

"Yes. Money's made to be spent, right?"

The journalist nodded, half-smiling, not knowing what an appropriate response might be.

"On all that 'poetry'"—he made air quotes with his fingers—"as Stevenson called it. That's where most of it went in those days."

"So you were quite the avid soul."

Bernard had no idea that the journalist didn't know he was alluding to all the wine, the "bottled poetry" he used to drink. He decided not to pick up on her reference to being an "avid soul." Probably one of the younger generation's buzzwords.

"And did you do this your entire working life?"

"I'm still working, young lady. I'm busier than ever!"

"Apologies. Let me put it another way. Have you been doing this work for a long time?"

"Love came my way, and, with it, a man's obligation to pass on his lessons to the next generation."

"David?"

"Well steady on. Hold your horses. David didn't just pop into the world. I had to meet his mother first. You do know that this whole thing about cabbage patches isn't true?"

The journalist could think of nothing she wanted less than a conversation with Bernard about making babies.

"It was love at first sight. For her."

"Let me guess. You had a lot of women to choose from."

"Well, aren't you the smart one? Yes, indeed, there were other suitors, or suitresses"—he chuckled at his clever little coinage—"who had me in their proverbial sights. I was a sporty young fellow with a higher-than-average income—*much* higher, in fact, given my age at the time."

"How old were you?"

"Not even thirty—and my bonus was already higher than the annual income of the prime minister." Bernard laughed out loud at his own remark—so loud that after thirty seconds he still took quite some time to take a sip of water.

"So she had to go all out to snag you in her net, if I understand correctly."

"It wasn't quite that hard. I didn't want to make things *too* tough for her. And besides, she soon turned out to be quite the suitable partner. I had asked her to an office dinner, and my managers were very positive a day later. And the ladies at reception seemed to be quite jealous."

The journalist uttered a low, skeptical "Hmmm," and then masked it by clearing her throat.

"At the time, it was customary to get married fairly quickly—and we also wanted to quickly take advantage of the tax benefits of marriage. We were married in southwest London with more than two hundred guests in attendance. We did it in the winter, so the venues were much better priced, and we knew we wouldn't be disappointed by the weather. I mean, the English winter can be really abominable."

"And days like that always feel warm, don't they?"

Bernard thought it was a strange interruption, but he smiled out of politeness. "Lydia, my wife at the time, wanted a big family. She had assumed that I did too since I was the youngest of five children.

"But this turned out not to be true?"

"Having more than one child was, and still is, regarded as antisocial behavior. A child is a duty; one needs an heir, and it would be inappropriate not to be able to pass on my knowledge and prosperity. Having more than one child is cumbersome. It causes a hassle with the inheritance, and the world population was rising fast even then. In addition, when David was born, it soon became clear that another year of such nights would not be conducive to my professional ambitions."

"You helped a lot as a father."

"My wife was a full-time mother, but I tried to contribute where I could, even though I had no choice in those years but to sleep a lot in a hotel right next to the office. There could be no question, of course, of my clients being disrupted by my private life."

"That must have been quite something."

"Indeed," he said, rather too curtly.

"But David had a good childhood then."

"I could not tell him that often enough. By contrast with my own childhood, everything was arranged for him, and he wanted for nothing. For his birthdays, we had clowns and a private bouncy castle for him and his friends. When he was seven, he asked for an electric train. We gave him not only the basic set and not only one extension set but two. He had a childhood free of any care in the world. Really lived like a prince."

"And you were the king."

"Ha ha—don't I wish. I worked relentlessly to pay for all this. In the meantime, I had started my wine collection, and the place had become so spacious that one maid was not enough. You know how it goes."

"Do I indeed. Such is life."

The journalist thought back to the only house on the street without a TV where, until she was eighteen, she'd shared a room with her sister who was seven years younger.

"When David was young, I saw little of myself in him. He had no interest in sports and certainly not in school. I blamed myself. He had it far too good, and he also had a role model whom it was difficult to live up to."

"Role model? Ah yes—sorry, of course."

"Yes, of course. Imagine what it must have been like to have a father like that. I tried to emphasize my shortcomings to him whenever possible, but it seemed in vain. It was difficult to get him out of his room. At one point I had arranged through a good colleague for our sons to be friends. When he came to play with us, it turned out after a few hours that the boy was alone on our trampoline while David was in his room staring at one of his cartoons."

"What kind of stuff was he looking at?"

"No idea. I just wanted to get him away from all that rubbish. Do you think I was doing that stuff as a child? In my time, we used to play hide-and-seek and football in the streets. We made each other stronger by competing. I knew I would have to intervene—and fast."

"Intervene?"

"I had to make a man out of him. Conscription had already been stopped, and boarding schools were, and still are, overpriced. So I put him to work. Through an old friend, he got a job at a law firm down the road. He was allowed to do all kinds of jobs there, and he immediately came into contact with good people."

"Lawyers? 'Good people'?" The journalist meant this as a joke. Bernard looked at her questioningly. She let it go.

"For years, he worked for Argew and Phibbs—a top-drawer firm. It showed him what a man has to do to take care of himself and, later on, his family."

"Well he has certainly put that lesson into practice."

"Yes, yes. I must admit, I initially had a different path in mind for him."

"I understand that. You're not really the enterprising type yourself, of course."

"I beg your pardon. I've always filled my roles at the bank in a most entrepreneurial way, young lady."

The journalist said nothing; it was clearly not worthwhile comparing his entrepreneurial skills with those of an actual entrepreneur.

"I thought it would be wise for him to work for a good company. Preferably close to the money, of course."

"Banks, right?"

"Exactly." Bernard was glad that he had been listened to.

"But it was not to be."

"David said at an early age that he would quit school as soon as the law allowed him to. It was a big worry—a very big worry. Especially when he went to live with his mother, and I had less and less influence on his education."

"You are divorced?"

"My wife at the time wanted a simpler life. She had found a man elsewhere who spoke more at her level. It was hard for her to keep up with me. She felt out of place around me and my peers. I should have known—she'd never been to university. She'd had only a vocational education."

"What did she study, if I may ask?"

"I have forgotten what exactly. Something to do with tourism, as I recall, or maybe it was languages. In any case, it was not the example I had in mind for David, and that new man certainly wasn't either."

"He didn't have a good degree either?"

"Ha! I wonder to this day whether he'd got any education at all."

"And are they still happy together?" Only a second later did the journalist realize that she'd taken a bit of a risk in asking that question.

There were a few moments of silence. Bernard took a sip of water. "You clearly haven't done your homework. Lydia has left us."

The journalist felt rather awkward for a few moments and found it difficult to find the right words.

"Unfortunately, he's still in the land of the living. If I'd had a choice between the two . . ." Bernard recovered and gave a little rolling wave with his right hand that meant the journalist could go on. He assumed there would be other questions. Fortunately, the journalist picked up on this.

"But you still saw David, and you could point the way forward for him."

"Fortunately, we still had time together, and I tried to make use of every minute of it. For him, and for his future."

"You went out together?"

"Sometimes, but mainly I brought him into contact with good role models. I asked many friends from my student days to have lunch with him and sometimes to even let him tag along for a day. Unfortunately, it didn't do much good."

"Unfortunately indeed. And now he's had to make do with the biggest exit of the last five years."

The witty remark was to no avail.

"Don't get me wrong. What David has done in the end is phenomenal. Fortunately, the laws of genetics also apply to him. It was not an easy path, but we were able to find something for him to do. Entrepreneurship was a nice solution that allows him to use his talents without needing the papers to be able to compete in the top tier, for example. He would have had no chance there."

"So you gave him a push toward entrepreneurship, as it were."

"I have primarily given him a safety net. I let him know almost every month that, if he changed his mind, or if he couldn't make it financially, I had a room for him and could put him in touch with friends for a nice start with a serious business."

"A serious business?"

"You sound just like David. That's not how I meant it. A company with a track record in a major industry. Institutions that can offer a nice path, a pension, and, eventually, nice conditions. Not to mention a less lonely existence."

"You worry about his social life."

"There was reason to anticipate success eventually, but the life that boy led during the first years was inhuman. I did not see him often, but when I did, it was not pleasant to be seen with him. He looked very unkempt—you smelled him rather than saw him coming."

They laughed together, though one of them did so out of politeness.

"When there was some indication that his concept could catch on, I offered him funding. No small amount, and for just a small piece of equity. Nothing compared to the deals I'd been accustomed to making. He turned it down. He turned everything down. He had to do, and would do, everything himself. Once I saw him on the square in front of the local supermarket handing out flyers and explaining to people how his concept worked. He even tried to convince close acquaintances not to buy their food in that supermarket but to join him. An acquaintance came up to me a few weeks later and told me. I said then, and have maintained ever since, that it was not David."

"Weren't you as proud as a peacock?"

"You misunderstand me again. The end result makes me very proud indeed, but someone with David's background should be more respectful with the hours he keeps—especially his working hours. I have a lot of respect for men—and nowadays women too—who sell things in person. But in their case, they simply haven't had the choice."

"You think that with his background, David is obliged to have an office job."

"The boy has developed a great brain, and he owes it to society to make the most of it. He's duty bound to turn his intelligence into output that not everyone can produce so he can then be rewarded for it. Leave the lowlier chores to the butchers, the bakers, the newspaper hawkers. And I mean that with all due respect, of course."

"Of course." For the first time, the journalist doubted whether she should allow this man any time on her carefully curated channel.

"It was only when David started to scale up that we really saw him hit his stride. At the opening of a new location in southern Germany, where I happened to be with my literary group, I saw him addressing some of his staff. He tried in German. Unfortunately he had not developed this *Fertigkeit* as far as I had, but, fortunately for him, he quickly switched to English. It was all very technology related, but he had his audience in the palm of his hand."

"You see him primarily as a leader then."

"He comes from a long line of visionary men. We're all strategists; we plot out the big picture and let the common man follow."

"In an interview, he once said that he did not see himself as a boss but as an employee who happened to have given the first push."

"Ha ha! That's so brilliant, isn't it? To think that I've managed to pass on my modesty to him, notwithstanding our other differences."

"Yes, fantastic." Once again, the journalist found it hard to hide her sarcasm.

# 3. NATASHA

Natasha absentmindedly picked up the empty cups and the half-filled pizza boxes. She used to complain loudly, doing everything she could to let everyone know that she was cleaning up, even though she hadn't helped organize the party or been part of it. Every morning when someone would happen to get out of bed early, she'd stress that she got up on time every morning because she no longer had the benefit of parental or other support. She had to pay for it all herself.

For two years now, she'd been telling anyone who'd listen, and even those who wouldn't, that she was leaving the dorm. As soon as the right flat came available and the bank cooperated, she'd be off—she'd left that life behind years before.

Even though she had climbed up to *the* room in the building—it was often called the penthouse, even though it was on the middle floor—it bothered her more with each day that passed that she had to share the front door with boys and girls, some of whom were almost a decade younger and were at a far earlier stage in their lives.

While the others would sometimes study for a while when exams were approaching but were mainly "developing socially," she would get on the same bus at the same time almost every day, usually six days a week, with the same bag, which had the same things inside it.

Even if this rhythm had been absent for a time, it had changed her. She had other goals, less time, and, most importantly, a different outlook on life.

She didn't want to admit it, but she looked down a bit on the others. She was aware that she'd been like they were not so long ago, but she was not proud of that. Now that she was taking care of herself and "adding value to society," she was prouder of herself. When asked if she was happier, she had no real answer. "Haven't given it any thought yet," she would say.

For a moment, she thought it was going to happen. All her hard work was going to be rewarded. When it became clear that the company she worked for would be taken over, there was euphoria for weeks at the office.

Colleagues joked about all kinds of hypothetical purchases. Brochures showing BMWs, Ferraris, and Porsches came in the mail. The faces of some managers were photoshopped onto unknown models with fur coats, and someone had even ordered a whole new Italian kitchen, which did not have to be paid for until eighteen months later. "That's pocket change," he'd said with a smile.

On just about any Monday, a group of consultants even younger than she was would ask whether they could sit down with her for an hour or so. They were very interested in what she did on a given day, her responsibilities, and what she thought could be improved.

There hadn't been an official end to the conversations, but one of them had asked with some interest about her time at the company. She felt a connection, she said, and wanted to know how Natasha felt about her first experience in the world of work.

At the consultant's expense, they'd gone to eat a few streets away at a new poke bowl place, which they said was the fourth best within a half-mile radius.

The consultant had ordered a poke bowl with a choice of no more than twelve ingredients. After she'd made her choices, there were five options left over. And still she paid the full price—something Natasha had never done. Natasha even considered adding the five remaining ingredients to her own order.

"So you're one of the veterans of RoboWok?"

"And still no gold watch." Natasha found herself very witty for a moment.

"How many of you were there when you started?"

"I was number four. David was there, of course. He had Dimitri from the start. At first, though, Dimitri was rewarded mainly with promises and free food, and not long before I started, Rakesh had also begun. I think that, to this day, he has never been near a machine that sells real food; he sees them only in 'the lab' he built at home."

"At home?"

"In the south of India. David is the only one who has ever seen him in person."

"Even though he's the *chief engineer*?"

"Well, he and Dimitri, but Dimitri said talking via WhatsApp and sometimes a video call is more than enough. He said great minds think alike."

"Are they both great minds, or is there actually just the one technical genius?"

It was at that moment that Natasha became aware that the girl, even though she was perhaps a year younger than she was, was still a consultant, and that she was probably out to learn more about who was talented enough to be keep on and who wasn't.

"They're both really brilliant."

Everyone knew that it was only after Rakesh had joined that there was actually a machine. Dimitri was there from the start, but almost everyone knew that David was not very happy with him and that it was too expensive to manage him.

"David and Dimitri built the first MVP together to test the concept."

"MVP?"

"Minimum viable product—the most basic version possible, created to test whether consumers were really waiting for such a concept."

"They put together the first RoboWok?"

"You could call it that. When we get back to HQ, I can show you some photos. I wouldn't expect too much. Have you ever been to a zoo or amusement park that has those panels with the figures drawn in but the face cut out?"

"Where you can stick your face through for a photo?"

"Yes, those. That was RoboWok version one. Internally, we call it the RoboMock. At the time, David rented an empty shop for a week. It was one of those locations normally intended for pop-up restaurants. In fewer than forty-eight hours, they'd put up a wooden shell in front of the shop with a little glass door in it. If you looked through the glass door, it looked as though a machine was moving the wok and throwing ingredients into it, but behind the hatch, the wok, and an extra layer of wood, David and Dimitri were preparing ready-made wok meals. They'd actually put buttons in the wood, but they weren't connected to any-thing. David just had to see which buttons were pressed in order to determine which meat and which sauce Dimitri should put in the wok."

"And no one caught on that it wasn't a machine at all?"

"Ha ha, yes. Most people did eventually figure it out. But not when they were buying their meals, and that was the whole idea."

"I don't understand. Wasn't the idea that they wanted to test a prototype?"

"No. The whole point of the MVP phase was to check whether people would buy a wok meal from a machine. Before that, there were vending machines, and you could also get food from little heated spaces in walls, but something like RoboWok, where the meal was cooked on the spot and on demand by a robot—that was quite new at the time."

"So there was no machine at all at that time—nowhere at all?"

"Dimitri was working on it, but it was only when Rakesh . . ." Natasha bit her tongue. She didn't want to give the consultant too much information about Dimitri's skills. She liked him. Dimitri did not add much, at least according to David, but he was always there. And especially during events, such as Halloween, he was always one of the movers and shakers. A few months earlier, he had turned up as the Beatles. Actually, he had been Ringo Starr, and he had had John, Paul, and George next to him. They had been puppets. At the beginning of the evening, when he had still been up for it, you could ask him to sing a Beatles song. Then, the heads of the dolls had moved in unison with Ringo's head. Natasha had also done her best. Once, she had been dressed up as Marilyn Monroe, even doing an act where her dress had blown up over the subway grating, with all the risk that entailed. However, that hadn't been a patch on John, Paul, George, and Dimingo. "In any case, the point is that they knew the world was ready for it. They were not so worried about building the machine."

"That's understandable in itself. Building a machine is under your control, whereas what the consumer wants is not."

Natasha was impressed by this girl and had enough self-awareness to know that she herself would not have caught on so quickly—or at least not to the point where she could articulate things so well.

"And did a lot of people eat at version one that week?"

"All the newspaper articles and many of the receipts are hanging in the wall by the coffee machine in the office. After people had received their wok meal from 'the machine,' if there was time, David would come out with a machine to take payment. This way, he could ask people how they liked RoboWok and also try out different prices directly with consumers."

"But that price was communicated in advance, wasn't it?"

"They did that with a white marker on the glass door in front of the wok, and they'd change it all the time. For years they bragged about the price elasticity they calculated in their heads while preparing the wok meals."

"That price was revolutionary, especially for the quality that was offered."

"David had calculated that they would have to incur far fewer costs. Smaller floor areas, no staff, better algorithms for calculating how many vegetables and how much meat, rice, and noodles were needed each day, and even a price that they could adjust per machine, per micro-second in case the machine was threatening to run out of stock."

"The dream of every restaurant owner."

"They didn't see that at first. That came much later. The whole restaurant world, especially when it started, agreed that humans would be better cooks forever and ever and that you have to test ingredients by hand, piece by piece."

"But at RoboWok, the machine does this."

"People supply the machine, but then the machine knows exactly what the best preparation is based on weight, temperature, customer preferences, and other inputs—much better than a human chef ever could."

"But people can taste."

"The software the machines use continually optimizes the combination of ingredients, the temperature, how well done the meal is, and other values so as to get the highest level of customer satisfaction. And on top of that, all these price advantages mean we can afford the best ingredients—something none of our competitors could ever manage."

"How cool to have been a part of this. It sounds better than reorganizing companies and prioritizing new business initiatives in endless spreadsheets." The consultant was shocked by her own honesty; she did not think this was professional on her part.

"Yes and no. Don't get me wrong, part of me is proud that I've contributed in my own way to a great change in the world . . ."

"An enormous change in the way people get their food!

"Yes, that's right. But when I started, I was responsible, among other things, for answering media and customer complaints. At least all the media that didn't want to film. David wanted to do that himself."

"He's the face of RoboWok."

"Yes, exactly. But most of the questions and requests came from customers and other media. There were a lot of people who were angry about what we were doing to the labor market."

"Jobs?"

"Back then, many more people worked in restaurants. As waiters and waitresses, in the kitchens, cleaning and washing dishes . . ."

"And they saw then what was going to happen?"

"At first, it was mainly certain people in the media, but their articles got more and more coverage, especially when we started growing really fast in certain cities. We pretty much became the face of the new industrial revolution, but this time without new jobs."

"Ah yes, I can remember something like that indeed." The consultant did not seem to feel any emotions on the subject. "How did you answer all those complaints? That seems like a really challenging first role."

"I remember my first day. I had no idea. Fortunately, David was still around, and we quickly decided on the many advantages we could parlay."

"Such as?"

"Price for the consumer, better ingredients, direct purchasing from local farmers, less waiting time, more consistent quality . . ."

"And this worked?"

"Not really, the media mainly kept going with profiles of people who lost their jobs 'because of us.'" Natasha had initially felt guilty about the consequences of her employer's actions. However, just as she was on her umpteenth day at the end of her tether, David had come up to her and talked about how progress always involved pros and cons, about the fantastic consequences of the first industrial revolution. Perhaps most importantly, though, he'd said that without him and RoboWok, someone else would've come up with a similar idea, and that at least they were doing things in the fairest way possible.

"Did it affect the business?"

"I have never experienced a day without growth. We even had days when we lost certain machines for a few hours because of breakdowns, but we still had growth from new machines and new customers."

"That's pretty astonishing."

"You're telling me."

"And all four of you did this?" The consultant already knew the answer but tried to seem impressed.

"Yes—us and an army of robots."

The consultant didn't press the point. She'd spent a lot of time looking at organograms, and she knew how many people had worked behind the scenes. However, she had also calculated the number of staff working per machine and the level of turnover and had briefly doubted whether her own job would be viable going forward.

"Would you like something else to eat or drink?" the consultant asked Natasha.

"No, thanks. I've had enough, really. And with my salary, I have to stop here." Natasha said it ostensibly as a joke, but she was actually hoping to make sure that the lunch would be paid for.

"Oh, don't worry, I'll get it."

"Oh, thanks so much. I hope someday I'll easily be able to get lunch for both of us."

"Yes, maybe so."

# 4. DAVID

"After this, you can never go back." At least that's what they'd told David. He had become a platinum member straight away; he saw no reason to become a member and not have access to everything.

He'd also been there the week before, mainly because he couldn't sleep, and it seemed as though he'd binge-watched everything on Netflix. He'd ended up among a group of white men, all at least twenty years older. They'd recognized him. One of them, the smallest and the fattest, who was also talking the most, had offered him a "real" Cohiba Behike. He'd said he didn't smoke—that he never had and never would—but the men had kept at him so much that somehow, a few minutes later, he was standing with a lit cigar in his mouth.

"And? Incomparable taste, am I right?"

Ten gray beards stared at David as he reluctantly—actually, unwillingly—took a puff from the cigar.

"It's really . . ."

"Yes?" The men looked at David hopefully, yearning for confirmation that the next generation of rich people would also understand that the cigar is *the* symbol of success.

". . . just as much of an overrated experience as I thought it would be."

The men left, disappointed, agreeing among themselves that taste comes with age and that the new generation just couldn't appreciate the finer things life had to offer.

"You could also have said it's just not for you."

A slightly younger man, though still probably more than ten years David's senior, was standing next to him.

"To make friends?"

"They are all men of influence. In here, but certainly outside too."

"Suppose I had invested in a relationship with them by lying. And suppose that this, after many cigars and other lies, had led to access to their network. What could that have achieved?"

"Influence, a place at certain tables, introductions that others would not get."

"You mean with companies, investors, politicians?"

"For instance." The man winked in a way that was quite sympatico—not off-putting or patronizing.

"And suppose through those friendships I made here, through lies, I were to get a seat at the table in these companies, with politicians and so on. What then?"

"Then you have access to information, deals . . ."

"To what end?"

"Aha, I see." The man put his glass down, directly on a glass table not far from several coasters or other options to protect the glass.

"You're already *in,* so you don't really need any more money. So you're fine. Is that it?"

David looked up. He did not expect to meet anyone in this environment who could formulate that kind of insight so quickly.

"The goal doesn't have to be more ownership, more memberships, or more power."

"What goal did you have in mind then?"

"You're asking me the 64,000-dollar question—a question that has occupied humankind for hundreds, perhaps thousands, of years. The meaning of life. And maybe that's what it comes down to. But maybe I'm looking for a more practical layer that's floating above it, as it were?"

"Yes, I understand. I know roughly what you sold for. And don't get me wrong—I don't even come close. But still, you're young, and you're *in.* You don't have to work and you'll never have to look at what something costs. And now you're thinking, what's next?"

"I will admit that I had not seen this conversation coming a few minutes after being surrounded by a very clichéd situation where gray-haired old men wanted to smoke cigars with me in an environment with Chesterfield armchairs and all those heraldic shields on the wall."

"You have to learn not to look down on them."

"I don't look down on them!" Even David felt he was overreacting.

"You do. You think the things they do and talk about are shallow and that what they care about is trivial."

"So you'd call smoking cigars, sitting on committees, and owning several houses important?"

"Exactly my point—you look down on them. Whereas you should be jealous of them."

"Jealous?"

There was a moment of silence. David was not used to such a probing exchange with someone he didn't know. "No, really, I don't understand why I should be jealous. Should I also start smoking cigars, collecting old cars, and wasting my time in all kinds of unimportant clubs?"

"That is not my point. The jealousy has nothing to do with how they spend their time. The essence is that they find their meaning—or at least I hope so for their sakes—in things like that. You have to lie awake every night mulling over big questions, while they solve everything with the swipe of a card."

It was too early for David to say it to this person he'd only just met, but these were the wisest words he'd heard, maybe ever. He dug into his memory but could recall only good business advice and tips for getting cheap kitchens and deals on car repairs. Life lessons of this order from a fellow human being were something new.

"It's only recently that I've been kept awake with questions like this. I was simply too busy with everything. If I had a moment to think about life, I would often fall asleep right away, or someone would pop in with an urgent question."

"Some people live their lives without these kinds of questions because they're always busy."

"Or just contented."

"They are the ones to be envied. That said, this is unfortunately the disadvantage of your talent."

"Talent?" David tried to appear modest, but he just managed to appear awkward.

"A good set of brains, good health, a good education, more than enough of a safety net to try one or another thing without financial pressure, and so on. Now, how many people on earth were given *that* at birth? Only benefits, except for one thing."

"Dying without having answered that question."

"Self-actualization."

"Maslow?"

"How many boys and girls of your age know immediately that I am talking about Maslow? I'm sure it's not because you are brilliant or all that well read."

"Purely what I was born into."

"Yes—your social environment, your genes."

"It sounds like you've been through this yourself." This was the first moment that David wanted to learn something about the stranger, even though it didn't feel for the time being as though he needed to know his name.

"I'm still going through it. Every day."

"And no answer at all. Pretty encouraging."

"I didn't come here to make you feel good about yourself. I was mainly talking about your behavior toward the club of men who very kindly offered you a hard-earned cigar, only to get that very nice thank you from you. It's like they say: no good deed goes unpunished."

"Not very nice."

"Certainly not. Now don't get me wrong— being liked by those men won't give you the answers you're looking for, but perhaps it will lead to experiences or to other people that *will* bring you closer to an answer."

"The same answer you haven't found for years despite all your searching."

"I'm not actively looking. I never really have been. I'm cheating."

"Religion?"

"Ha ha, no. Denial. Though it's not much different. I just started doing things, keeping myself busy."

"In this kind of club?"

"I think I'm not managing to make myself clear." The man kept the same patient tone, despite David's somewhat recalcitrant attitude. He also seemed to be looking at the same spot on a far-off wall the whole time.

"Sorry—you're talking here to people who help you answer life's biggest question?"

"Something like that."

# 5. MARIA

Not a day went by without Maria's coming across a new object—more often than not electronic—of which its intended use she didn't know.

She'd always had tools in her life: a clothesline, a comb, a mat beater. She couldn't live without them, but she couldn't really think of any other activities in her life for which she might want to have tools.

She'd always enjoyed solving things with her hands, even if there was an automated solution. With age came the realization that she was just like her mother, and her mother's mother, even though she had chosen to live with new ground under her feet. Washing machines were never something for them, and everything in the kitchen was done with the same small potato peeler.

Maria had recently been walking around in a house in which she still felt she had not seen every room. So much wealth, so many places to fill with things that fulfilled purposes she couldn't imagine.

Her new boss, who was really quite young, had insisted that she use certain machines. Otherwise she would've done everything with a few simple tools.

It wasn't that Maria wasn't happy with what she had. It was just that she could think of much better uses for the money she didn't have— and almost certainly never would have. When no one was around, she would take a moment to daydream about all the possible uses for it. Traveling back home once a year, a new car for her father, an extra pair of gym shoes for her son, and being able to say yes when he asked to go to football camp every year.

Maria's husband promised her almost every day that all these dreams would soon come true. Every day he had a business plan, a job opportunity he was perfect for, or a friend who had an opportunity for him that could not be missed.

Maria promised herself to always be positive. She always managed to remember, amid all the rejections, that he was at least trying. With a smile, she cleaned up the area around him, always smiling kindly at his friends who would sit at her table drinking her salary, without wiping their feet or thanking her for all the meals she served them with love.

She didn't have it so bad. Her new employer took good care of her. She had never worked on the books or gotten so many perks on top of her salary. For the first time, she was insured and actually had her pension paid into a company whose name she could not remember, no matter how hard she tried.

Another first was that, in her second week, her new boss had actually taken the time to find her and give her a nice welcome. She hadn't known who this approaching figure might be, but a colleague called out to her just in time. She quickly straightened her outfit, put her hair up, and donned the best smile she could manage.

At the very last second, she saw a fleck at the bottom of her apron. She tried to crumple up the bottom quickly to hide it, but just as she was doing that, she heard, "Good morning."

In front of her was a kid. That's what he was—a kid. Unshaven, in a black T-shirt with all kinds of rather lugubrious images on it, probably from some band. She guessed he was no more than ten years older than her son.

"Good morning, sir." Those were the words she'd been practicing a lot. Her hope was that nothing too much more complex in the way of a conversation would have to follow.

"Welcome to the family. My name is David."

"Many thanks for being my employee. Sorry, oh, please excuse me, sir. I meant 'employer.'" All that practice clearly hadn't done any good.

"Ha ha—no problem. It's great to be able to do something for you, ma'am."

"Oh please—no need to be formal, sir."

"Well, all right, then—but only if you don't keep calling me 'sir' either!"

"As you wish, sir. Sorry, I mean, 'As you wish.'"

"Yes—it's David. Do you have everything you need? And do you know where to find the tea and coffee?"

"Yes, David. Thank you, si—. Thanks. I've got everything I need. I'll make sure you always have a nice house. I won't leave before it's spotless."

"I trust that you'll do a good job and that you'll make sure you have everything you need to perform well."

"Oh, what kind of performance?"

"Oh, I just mean the cleaning."

"Oh, should I perform while I'm cleaning? Like singing or something."

"Ha ha, no just cleaning is fine. By 'perform well,' I just meant 'clean well'—that you should make sure you have whatever you need to do your job as best you can."

"Oh, sorry, sir."

"No 'sir.'"

"Oh, sorry. David."

Those had been the few minutes, which flew by like a few seconds, with the boss—an almost meaningless exchange that, for all that, had made a big impression.

It had made her especially paranoid. She had heard many stories about rich people who were very kind to your face but who were actually stingy and made their people work as hard as possible for as little as possible.

At home, she had told everyone about the encounter, and everyone saw it the same way she did. This had to be one of those cases. He definitely had someone who make sure everyone got squeezed for all they were worth.

"You mark my words. If you put a foot wrong even once—forget some little thing or ask to take a break—you'll be out on your ear before you know it." Everyone had nodded in agreement as if they'd all seen it hundreds of times before.

Every day before she went through the gates of the estate, she'd repeat that mantra to herself: *Think of the good conditions. Don't get distracted by all the friendliness. Don't screw up, Maria.*

The routine was the same; she'd go through the section of the house for that day. It was all on a laminated list drawn up by the head of housekeeping. She did everything in the order shown, all within the specified time with the things she was meant to use according to the same laminated list. If she finished a bit early, she'd look for something extra to do or clean a certain spot in places where no living creature would ever go.

Perhaps the best part of the job was that the list consisted of nine sections. Each section was made for a full working day. This meant that all staff had new surroundings each day for nine working days. Maria had her favorite areas, especially the bowling alley with the lane machine, and spending a morning fishing stuff out of the swimming pool with a scoop net didn't really seem like work to her. She'd even have done it just for fun.

Every day, she'd walk toward the bus physically satisfied, but then mental fatigue would start to set in. She had learned to love being physically tired. She saw it as a much-needed way to save on pricey gym memberships, and it kept her from lying awake too long in bed at night.

The best thing would be if she never lay awake again, but, unfortunately, the mind was often stronger than the body on that score. She made lists and kept track of all the outgoing cash, especially to see if there might be any expenses she could put off till the next month.

She had managed to get a lot of costs under control. They got their TV signal via a digital aerial. Rent increases were still limited. They switched energy suppliers every year. Things like shampoo and toothpaste were bought in bulk every six months, depending on the promotions, and with a huge trove of coupons clipped from free newspapers.

Everything she could get under control, she'd gotten under control. When her husband was still working, he would always say, "He who pays the piper calls the tune." Unfortunately, that didn't seem to hold in this new situation. Sometimes the week would seem to go by without any unnecessary expenses, but then in one "exceptional evening," as he'd call it, he'd go way over his budget in some bar or other.

For a while, they had worked together somewhat successfully, when certain debts became so large that men who were bigger with each subsequent visit appeared at the door every day. It seemed that most of them were wearing the same jacket. It seemed that it was not the debts that would get her husband up and out of the house early but the prospect of the early-morning visits from these bailiffs.

And that's how he'd found the job that seemed to guarantee they'd soon be out of the woods. But the extended celebrations her husband had launched into—and those went on for almost a week—had brought them pretty much back to square one. It had taken her almost a month to get over this. She took the discount bouquet he gave her in the third week as a peace offering and decided, as she always did, to stay positive.

This month wasn't looking good either. Once again, there was a shortfall, partly because of her husband's nights out the week before. She would have to get yet another credit card so she could pay off a short-term debt by incurring a slightly longer-term debt. She had become very skillful at all of this by now, even though clicking OK or signing a contract hurt more and more each time.

Every last Friday of the month, she would speak to her father on a video call. Her father would be in his local cybercafé, a legacy of the previous millennium. They would call to check in on each other. She called it "checking in" on purpose: her father would have balked at any other way of putting it. He did not want to be "babysat," and certainly not from another continent.

Her father was in many ways the love of her life. She had even made peace with the fact that she would never know a greater love—only her son still stood a chance, if he kept on the straight and narrow.

It was now mostly old men who were living in the village she came from. All the younger men had already left for centers of work and opportunity. The old men filled their days with card games and stories of the old days. It was the same scene in most villages in the region. All men of a respectable age lived like this—except her father.

Her father did not see his golden years as a time to start playing cards, and certainly not to look back. He had always seen himself as an inventor. The years he'd spent working were, he said, "just an interlude."

It was one of her greatest blessings, and also one of the few she had. Her father wanted to know everything about everything and, if at all possible, by building everything himself. He spent half of his time collecting rubbish—public gold, as he used to call it—and the other half repairing and/or transforming it. It generated little income, but that was no longer necessary. What it achieved above all, especially for Maria, was the right kind of curiosity and a willingness to speak to her online each month. None of the men she once called her uncles, even though they were not related, had ever used the internet. No one except her father, who used the internet for three things and nothing else: to call her, to discover new processing techniques and, where possible, to get some much-needed cash from his only daughter.

She had never planned to live so far away from her father. Money was the only reason she did. It was hard to come by locally. Her husband had convinced her father that they could both earn much more in another part of the world for the same work. The higher cost of living there had not yet occurred to either of them.

So there she was on the other side of the world with debts that were bigger than she could ever have imagined and that completely overshadowed the much higher salary she was now getting.

Her greatest motivation had not always been her son's football camp. It was an opportunity to give her father something back every month, something extra that would allow him to make the most of his remaining days. A small compensation for the loss of his daughter.

She'd had difficulties with the connection on her monthly call that Friday. After they had both hung up several times and tried again three minutes later, they had managed to get a connection that was just about good enough.

"Papi, there's something else I have to tell you."

"What is it, sweetie? I hope your health is OK and everything." Every time her father called her "sweetie," it made the little hairs on her arms stand on end.

"No, no, don't worry. We're all healthy. It's about our monthly contribution."

"Oh, I see. If it helps you, feel free to pause it."

"No, I want to help you out wherever I can. That's the least we can do."

"But why?"

"'Why? Because of everything you've given us! All those years, and all those investments you made in us, without any hope of anything in return."

"I made a conscious choice to be your father. That does bring with it obligations, but above all it has brought us so much joy—and it still does."

These beautiful words hurt Maria most of all. They made her feel guilty. She would've preferred to hear him get angry, but that never happened.

"Papi, we're going to make sure that in your old age, you don't have to think about trivial things like money."

"I'll be all right. The government has said it'll help us."

"Oh, Papi—the government and its big fat promises!"

"Come come, sweetie. There's nothing to be gained from all that pessimism."

"You're right. But until the government helps us, I want to make sure you don't have any financial needs."

"I can eat a little less, and I have plenty of projects going on."

"You have to eat what you want and as much as you want. Thanks to you, Mama and I have never wanted for anything."

"Sweetheart, you and Mama were the best reward for my work I could have ever hoped for. And anyway, don't worry about your Papi so much."

"How can I not worry? You're all alone there, and you're not getting any younger."

"Really, don't worry about me. I can still run the one hundred meters faster than many a young man from the city here."

"I know you can, Papi—I know."

"Remember that time you were almost late for your performance? You were eight, I think, and you were playing one of the Three Wise Men. I charged all the way to your school with you on my back and got there in less than five minutes. Remember?"

"I do, Papi." Maria was actually already ten, and she heard this story almost every month. It had been one of the most beautiful evenings of her life. Those minutes on her father's back, and especially those moments when she saw him rise to his feet and applaud her performance, had stayed with her ever since.

"That's nice of you, sweetie. It's great if you want to give your Papi a little something now and again, but honestly, I can do without it. Take care of yourself and of my grandson. I'll be fine."

"This is a one-off thing, Papi. And I've made a promise that I'll do it."

"Well it's a promise you came up with and that you made to yourself. Now don't get me wrong, sweetie. I'm touched. I really am. But your happiness is what really counts for me."

Maria fought back her tears. She didn't want to show any sign of weakness or let her father hear that the only place she wanted to be was with him. With each sweet word she heard, it became harder and harder to hold back her tears and sound calm and collected.

"How is my boy doing?"

"The coach says he's the best defender he's had in years."

"Just like his granddad."

"He misses you so much."

"And I miss you both, sweetie. But we can't have everything. I've had a fantastic life, and I've known the two most wonderful women in the world. You must make sure that you and my boy are just as happy."

"We are." It hurt Maria so much to lie like that. Again, she felt a lump in her throat, but she quickly told herself that this lie was best for everyone.

# 6. NATASHA

The door handle she had opened the door with every morning, without a thought, had been replaced by a stainless steel doorknob. She had pushed and knocked on the window several times, but the door was still closed.

She had woken up very early that morning, even though she had been binge-watching till all hours the night before. For more than an hour she'd tried to go back to sleep but had eventually given up the ghost.

She'd read the email once again on her phone. The subject line had stuck with her: "Day One is next week."

She was in two minds about this. There was a relatively positive thought: the new owner had looked at Jeff Bezos and had stolen the idea that every day is Day One. On the other hand— this was the negative thought—the new owner was acting as though Day One was actually the first day for RoboWok.

Natasha could sometimes be quite the prophet of doom. Weeks in advance of any sort of event, she could think through all kinds of worst-case scenarios and would imagine how she, the victim, could best get through them. Around her sixteenth birthday, there was a gala at her school. Everyone was looking forward to it and had been busy with all kinds of preparations for weeks beforehand. But not Natasha. She'd often isolate herself and would sometimes spy on girls and boys who might ruin her evening.

In this case, it already bothered her that the new owner would not look back on the real first day of RoboWok, the real Day One, and that her long history with the company would be meaningless to the new owners.

She had already envisioned the day, minute by minute, in her mind. All new people on their Day One. New people with job titles, in suits made of wool from Italian mountain villages she'd never heard of. They'd walk around as if they owned the place. As if they owned *her* place.

She would try to talk about their success story at the coffee machine—about the long nights and the stressful weekends. They would look right through her, showing not the slightest interest, and turn every conversation back toward themselves.

There'd actually been no indication at all that they'd do any such thing, but the mere thought that they would had kept her awake. And now here she was, standing in front of a closed door, which she used to be able to open with ease. It was an omen.

"Good morning."

Natasha was startled by this far-too enthusiastic greeting. Surely not the done thing at this time of day.

"You trying to get in?"

"Yes, I work here."

"Me too. Nice to have a new colleague." Again, Natasha thought the enthusiasm was misplaced, but she did her best to manage a smile.

"So you've come to help us?" Natasha emphasized the "us" in a rather unnatural way.

"Yes, I was also part of the preliminary process. But today we can really start the journey."

"The preliminary process?" Natasha was already visibly irritated by the fact that he was talking about a journey that was about to begin when she'd already been on the actual journey for quite some time.

"I led much of the due diligence before the acquisition. And you? From Google, or McKinsey maybe?"

"For me, this is not Day One."

"Oh, you're not Natasha by any chance?"

"How did you know?"

"I'm not allowed to say that much yet. Winifred wants to announce that sometime this week. However, I have a feeling that we'll be seeing a lot of each other in the near future."

This came across as disturbing and verging on creepy, especially from this unknown man standing there in the dark at this very early hour. Natasha forced a quick smile, and as soon as the door clicked open, she slipped inside. She made one beeline for the coffee machine, and then another for her seat.

"Oh, right, you also need a pass for that door, too. One sec—I'll be right there."

And once again Natasha found herself standing in front of another closed door that had a new lock on it and that had always been open before.

Through the little panes on one side of the door, she saw that her place was still there but surrounded by a lot of new desks and even more unpacked boxes.

"Here you go. You can request one of the passes on the intranet. The back office will help you so you can soon unlock these doors yourself."

"Nice of them." Natasha wasn't one for small talk—she wanted to get her coffee and

guard her spot. All sorts of scenarios were racing around in her head about the mysterious
disappearance of her belongings in the drawers
of her desk.

The still-nameless man held his pass in
front of a new device right by the door. After
a series of whirrs and clicks that lasted almost
three seconds, he pushed the door open.

*"Après vous, madame."*

Again, Natasha forced a smile. The man
let her pass but did not give her much room
in the doorway. Natasha went in awkwardly,
trying hard not to have any contact with him
or the doorpost.

"Don't worry. In the next few weeks, everything will be done and many of these people
will go to floors sixteen to eighteen."

"Three new floors?"

"Three extra floors. We're also working on
fourteen, but obviously we want to have fifteen, too."

"Of course."

Natasha walked to her seat, hung her coat over her chair, and checked all the drawers in her desk. Everything was still there, just where it had been.

However, two desks had been pushed up against hers—one facing it, the other on the right. The one on the right had a big pile of boxes stacked on it. Natasha took a look around. The coast was clear. Even though she was quite light, she decided to push the two new desks against an empty wall to give her desk the space it needed. *No one will notice*, she thought.

After an extra check on her belongings, including the polaroid hanging under her screen with a handwritten note on its thick white frame indicating where it had been taken, she went on her next trip to the coffee machine. Early on in the company's history, she had taken it upon herself to be in charge of the coffee. She had arranged the machines and ensured that there were always enough beans for the grinder. She had found a coffee-roasting house not far from the office, selected the beans, and made a deal.

To her horror, her machine was gone, and her coffee was nowhere to be found. There was a very large black machine with nine white buttons for different varieties of coffee and tea and two kinds of soup.

She had already imagined that this would happen. But it was even more disappointing than she'd feared as she'd lain in bed that morning. She promised herself to stay strong "as long as things don't get even worse."

She took a step toward the machine to look at the coffee options. Espresso, double espresso, black coffee, café creme, cappuccino. After a deep sigh, she decided to go for the cappuccino. She pressed the white button. Nothing happened. She pressed again and only then did she notice a small screen. She read, in poorly lit lettering, "fifteen cents."

"Would you like a cup?"

Natasha was once again startled by the guy with no name, who now fished a few coins out of the money compartment of his brown leather wallet.

"It'd be great if I could borrow some. I haven't had any cash on me for eons."

"Ha ha. Consider the loan a small gift. I can spare the fifteen cents."

The man put the coins into the machine. Together they watched as a plastic cup dropped out of the machine and was filled, first with some milk and then with a piddling stream of coffee.

"So is this going to be the new strategy? Making staff pay for the coffee?"

"Ha ha. That would be quite something. No, I think head office has some deal. These machines are at all the subsidiaries."

"Subsidiaries?"

"The conglomerate is huge. I've been in only a tenth of the locations, but this machine was in each one."

"Making this delicious coffee." Natasha had perfected her sarcastic tone at an early age.

"Ha ha. Well it serves its purpose."

Natasha walked back to her desk. It was now the only one that was not next to any other furniture on the packed work floor. She sat down and took a sip.

"Holy sh—eugh!"

From where she was sitting, she could hear her new colleague laugh.

Maybe drinking disgusting coffee together at this hour created something of a bond between them, but the way he'd talked about "the head office" and "the conglomerate" was even more disgusting than the coffee she'd just sipped.

Natasha opened her laptop, connected her monitor, and waited for everything to start up.

The desktop image that came up was new. It featured a logo she recognized from the internet when there were the first murmurings of a takeover.

Her name popped up after she entered the code she'd put in before. And for the umpteenth time, she also put in her old password.

A message appeared that read: "Username and password do not match."

Perhaps the "09" had become a "10" at the end of her password. She tried again.

"Username and password do not match."

Natasha tried at least ten other options, and then gave up the ghost. She saw that, apart from the desks and the boxes, the rest of the office floor was still completely empty. Her new colleague was nowhere to be found either.

After hesitating a few minutes, she decided to walk back toward the coffee machine. Next to this new eyesore of a machine, she'd seen a stack of papers with the rather inviting word "CONFIDENTIAL" stamped on them in red capital letters.

Natasha looked around her again. She called out, but not too loudly, "Hello? Anyone here?" No reply. She tried again. The place seemed to be quite empty.

She picked up the first document in the pile and began leafing quietly through it. The words "Day One" appeared on a lot of the pages, alongside financial statements and graphs with lines going up and to the right.

From the moment she picked up the document, she actually wanted to put it back down again. Objectively speaking, the risk of getting caught on Day One did not outweigh any information she might find.

Nevertheless, she decided to look at a few more pages, at a faster pace, having checked again to make sure there was no one else around.

She was just thinking she'd seen enough when she found a dozen or so pages of organograms. Bosses at the top, staff at the bottom. She recognized a few names on the first pages but kept searching for her own.

After looking at all the unfamiliar names, which seemed to come from just about every country in the world, she had still not found herself on the penultimate page.

It had to be on the last page.

She turned the page and saw, in a font slightly larger than was used for the previous titles, "Post-Acquisition Integration Team." Her finger moved from one box in the chart to another. And there it was, at the very bottom, next to a photo of her that had been taken before her time at RoboWok. The role she had been given was:

"Junior Workflow Specialist"

She thought back to her primary school years, when she'd be asked almost every month what she wanted to be when she grew up. Ballerina. Firefighter. Pop star. Ballerina again. Many professions had come up, but "Junior Workflow Specialist" wasn't one of them.

After a few minutes of letting everything sink in and checking again that she was alone, she looked again at the rest of the page.

Soon, the irritation at not understanding the job title was replaced with a much deeper frustration. Only now did she realize that her name was at the bottom of a pyramid. Above her name were not one but three more senior layers.

She couldn't help looking at the name directly above hers. She had seen enough of these kinds of reviews of RoboWok to know that this would probably be her supervisor.

"Karl von Frisch—Team Lead, Organizational Transition"

She took out her phone and Googled the name. A Nobel Prize winner who had discovered that bees dance.

She clicked through to the second page of search results and saw a freshly cut white guy, blond, with a neatly tied tie. He was looking sternly at the camera. In the background was a pale blue wall, presumably a screen that was meant to look like the sky.

She clicked on the picture and was immediately directed to an overview of his career so far. University of Salzburg. London School of

Economics. Eighteen months at a British bank up to the present.

She scrolled down and saw that he was interested in entrepreneurship, e-commerce, and digital marketing. There was a link to research he had done as a student—all very uninteresting.

She scrolled up again. University of Salzburg. London School of Economics. Eighteen months in a British bank up to the present.

She was dumbstruck. This Karl guy, after having worked for eighteen months in a bank, was going to be her boss. Not only had he been working for a shorter time, but at a bank to boot. An industry that couldn't care less about her RoboWok.

Natasha quickly put the document back on the pile. She had to leave the office. She couldn't let out her feelings here. She walked toward her desk, took her coat and her bag, and checked that all the drawers were closed.

She more or less stomped out to the door. She put her hand on one of the panes in the door and pushed. It was locked. To the left of the door another new device. She would need a pass.

She went back to her desk. Without taking off her coat, she put her bag on her chair and sat down on the edge of her desk.

She knew this Karl only from one small photo. She knew something about his background, but not too much. And already she could not help thinking that he would be a terrible person. She fantasized about how she could contrive to hear him as little as possible. How emails he would send could just keep failing to show up in her inbox. How she would accidentally make typos in his presentations to the new bosses.

Hmmm. The new bosses. She thought back to the "confidential" document. She could not suppress her curiosity. Who was Karl's boss? And who was *their* boss?

Not too loudly, she called out "Anyone there?" again.

No answer—and still no other indication that anyone else was around. She walked toward the new coffee machine again and up to the pile of documents, which she found very awkward to leave there, especially since they were supposed to be "confidential."

This time she was able to navigate very quickly to the page that had her name on it. Her finger followed the line upwards, to Karl. And then she kept going and saw "Head of Post-Acquisition Integration." *Oh my God*, she thought. Was a title like this to be her new life goal?

Once again, she Googled the name. Pablo De Solminihac. Apart from other Pablos with the same surname, there were not many search results. Natasha searched then images.

She was startled for a moment. The third image in a row of five was the guy with no name from that morning. She would never have put such a name to such a face.

The fifteen-cent guy, who had come here just as early as she had, was her boss's boss.

# 7. BERNARD AND DAVID

David's phone rang. It was Bernard.

"My son."

"Hello, father."

"I have some really great news for you!"

"Oh, do tell!" David had heard this enough times before to know that the "great" news could only be a disappointment. Unlike in his teenage years, he'd also had enough experience by now to know that making clear how low his expectations were would not produce a better outcome for anyone.

"Well, strictly between us—no one, but no one, should know that I'm telling you already, but—ready?"

"Don't leave me in suspense for a minute longer." David injected a bit of a giddy note into his plea, but he didn't want to overdo it lest he should come across as cynical.

"Right, then. My son, in the next few days, you'll be getting a rather special invitation—the kind that only gentlemen three times your age usually get."

"The Nobel Prize?"

"Oh now—don't be daft. And what would you do with that kind of thing anyway?"

"Yes, those Swedes with all their prizes." David noticed that he felt a bit of excitement at the thought of winning a Nobel Prize. His father's voice cut that moment short.

"You are going to be speaker of the month!"

There was a silence of well over ten seconds.

"Well then? Speaker of the month!"

"Father—sorry, but can you please give me a bit more information? Will I be on TV again? Or be interviewed on the radio?"

"Ha ha, no, young fellow. You get to speak in front of a completely different audience, the *crème de la crème.*"

Another silence, which seemed to last even longer.

"Crazy boy! You can come and talk at the club. Everyone will be there. Everyone will listen to you—to your story."

David couldn't imagine anything worse than this "great" news. His first impulse was to rip off the Band-Aid, to tell his father right then and there to forget it. But he didn't have the heart.

"Well that *is* quite an honor. Do we know exactly when it'll be?"

"Yes, it's fantastic. Probably on the last Tuesday of the month. Usually it's right after the soup is served."

An unbelievable custom. A large group of men would be served soup—soup that would have been carefully made by several hands during the day and, given who the audience were, made from ingredients that would also have received a lot of love. However, instead of eating the soup and appreciating its value, the men would be listening to a speaker who was expected to hold forth for quite some time so that in the meantime the soup would come to room temperature and hardly anyone would end up having it.

David quickly picked up a stack of papers and leafed through them so they would make a racket.

"I'm looking this minute at my calendar, father."

The last time David had had a paper diary was when he was thirteen, and even then, he hadn't used it. He assumed that this would be a detail that his father would not have saved on his hard disk.

"Whatever you have scheduled, my boy, just take it out and block off the day. There are many men who have been waiting for years for such an invitation. Some go to meet their maker before they ever get one."

"Well, perhaps it would be a nice gesture if I took someone off that waiting list."

"You're too good for this world, my boy. But no, take this chance. You've earned it."

Bernard hadn't been able to wait any longer before telling his son. He had known about the invitation for almost three weeks.

Wherever he could, he let other members know that something big was going to happen at the club that month. "You really shouldn't miss this month. The speaker we have lined up is really in a class of his own."

Bernard had even checked with the staff to make sure he would be sitting in just the right spot: at a table near the president and close to the middle, where the floor was raised slightly. Everyone would be able to see him there and make the connection between him and the speaker. And he'd already had his favorite suit dry-cleaned and had had new shoes made specially for the occasion.

He'd invited two other fathers to his table, who had sons around the same age—young men who'd studied in a different way than David had and then had gone on to work for reputable names. He had spent years hearing about their promotions, their deals, and in which media their names had appeared. Bernard had kept quiet most of the time. The fact that his son was setting up a fast-food restaurant—which is how he saw it—was something he'd thought would be better kept quiet.

When the time came for the lecture, everyone would see what he had produced. His DNA would be there for all to see. He had already practiced in the mirror how he would react to all the compliments. He had decided to go for the humble approach: "Oh well, you do what you have to as a father." *It would be the best outcome in terms of perception*, he thought. *People would be envious, and his show of humility would make him even more amiable.*

He would also go to the club for brunch the next morning, something he'd never done before. There would still be announcements that had been posted from the day before, and everyone would be reminded of what he had produced. He had also booked a table for the brunch, a table he would normally never book, close to the only passageway to the brunch hall. Everyone would have to pass him to get through.

"Father. What am I expected to talk about?"

"It's your moment, my boy!"

"So I can say what I want?"

"Ha ha. There is a lot of freedom, but it will be appreciated if the topic is at least somewhat close to the interests of the audience."

"Golf? The stock market?"

"Ha ha! Crazy boy! They want to know who you are, how you've gotten this far—what you've created, and what your new plans are."

"I can elaborate on the new industrial revolution, which means more and more jobs are being replaced by robots, and how, unlike before, there are no new jobs to be had. How this will have major social consequences. How we as the 'haves' should help the 'have-nots' and how we should distribute wealth. About the role of mone, and how the current way of distributing it will no longer work."

"Boy oh boy! It's supposed to be an enjoyable lecture. These men have plenty of serious issues in their lives. They want to enjoy their old age and what they have acquired. Don't get me wrong—those topics are indeed interesting but not for this audience."

"Ah. Well then, I can talk about the initial mission and the growth."

"And the exit."

"The exit?"

"I think everyone's really keen to know what you plan to do with the wealth you've accumulated for yourself. You can talk about the house you've built and perhaps about some of your investments."

"That wouldn't be much of a story." David took a sip of tea.

"Well then, talk about how you got this far, about your earlier years, when you noticed you were far more enterprising than your peers. And how together we strengthened this entrepreneurial character of yours."

David quickly put his hand over his phone and blurted out a loud guffaw. The sip of tea he had just taken came out of the corners of his mouth. "David, are you still there?" David recovered himself somewhat.

"Yes, father. I can certainly go into some detail about my entrepreneurial youth." David had to keep stifling his laughter.

"Ah, that's my boy. Do you remember we had that 'Bring Your Child to Work Day' at my office? I believe you had just become a teenager."

David remembered it quite well indeed. His father's work—in fact, everything about him—had been pretty much a mystery when David was young. That was the first and only day he had ever been in his father's office.

"Remember that session where we simulated a business?"

"Yes. I was responsible for handling the complaints."

"That's right. And you made a superb job of it. I'm convinced that's where we planted the seed."

"The seed of what, father?"

"Well that was a real turning point for you. Before that day, you had no interests, really no passion or purpose in your life, but from then on . . ." He stopped.

"'From then on what?"

"You were a different person. It would take some time, but it was obvious. It triggered something in you. Business, customer-centricity, profits, losses."

"A true game-changer, father." David looked at his options. He could say how he really felt or explain his complete lack of engagement and say that what he had seen that day had served only to increase his detachment from the business world. He quickly realized that this would not make anyone any happier.

It would break his father's heart, and he himself would feel guilty. After all, this was the man who had nurtured him, given him shelter, and occasionally told him during the holidays that he was doing certain things right, such as carrying groceries inside.

There was another silence as David pretended again to be rustling through his diary. In fact, he didn't need an agenda since he had very little to do in the coming weeks, or even months for that matter.

"Ahhh—the last Tuesday of the month, you said?"

"Yes, this month already. You don't have to wait too much longer."

"I have bad news, I'm afraid." David tried to come up with a watertight excuse in double-quick time.

"I have tickets for an American band, Elephant in the Room, that I've been dying to see for years now. They're kicking off their reunion tour at the Ryman in Nashville. It's going to be a great show, and everything's already booked."

It was painfully quiet on the other end of the line. David braced himself for what was coming next. Would his dad react angrily, pointing to everything he'd had to give up for his son? Would he talk about how, if he'd had no children, he could have been anything and seen anything—about how he'd made sacrifice after sacrifice, only to be treated as someone who always asks and never gives?

It was worse.

"David, my boy. It's not like I'm constantly asking you for things—and certainly not things like this. Maybe I don't deserve it. I know all your friends probably had better fathers. But I'm asking you, this one time, to do this for me."

The humility and the disappointment in his father's voice were heartrending. David had never heard anything quite like this from him before. A few attempts in the same ballpark, perhaps, but certainly nothing directed so forcefully at him.

David said nothing but loudly rustled some random papers again.

"You know what? I've just seen that they'll be headlining at Lollapalooza in Chicago two weeks later. Well that's a lucky one. I'm honored, father, and I'm looking forward to talking all about my journey and my life after the Robo-Wok exit."

"Well that's just fantastic, my boy. You're making your father really happy. Everyone will love your story."

"Oh, the pleasure's all mine."

"I'll send you some ideas later, OK? Perhaps it will help you put together something compelling."

"You do understand that I've talked quite a few times on this subject, in front of all kinds of audiences?"

"Yes, of course, but I'd like to make this one extra special. Don't worry—I won't send you any lame texts. Just some anecdotes. Some things we used to do together, things that I think have helped you along the way."

David was already regretting his decision. He had never regretted so much having to miss a nonexistent event.

# 8. MARIA

She always told herself not to pay attention to it—the way people looked at her. It was clear that, with every glance from a native inhabitant of her adopted country, there was a boatload of prejudice.

She did everything she could to make the stereotype a lie. She wore clothes identical to those worn by the mothers of the native pupils in her son's class. She did not use the shopping trolley that everyone from her country used, even though she wanted to. She mostly read domestic news from local newspapers.

She saw it as an essential part of the success of her new life and, more importantly, that of her son's. They couldn't remain outsiders. If they were to unlock the kinds of opportunities insiders had, they'd have to behave like insiders.

When she'd started her job, she'd also had mixed feelings. On the one hand, she was extremely happy with the security and the salary that came with it. It was more than she had ever felt able to expect. On the other hand, she briefly considered turning it down. Almost everyone who'd had this job and others like it was an outsider. Accepting it would thus go completely against her plan for success of becoming an insider.

So there was a brief moment when she was convinced that she should not do it. It would be a short-term prospect that would keep her from her long-term goal.

At the same time, it was as if all the entities she owed money to had sent their bills all at the same time. In one go, she had to come up with the annual top-up fees for school, pay for the extra gas she had used, pay the electricity and water bills, repay a tax refund she'd been given in error, and, as if all of that weren't enough, pay an old fine that she got a third reminder for, this time at the right address.

She'd spent a whole day on the phone, trying to negotiate the amounts down and, where possible, arranging to pay in installments. She had no luck getting the amounts reduced, but she was able to make payment arrangements in all but two cases. It was a small success. Still, it was clear that she had merely been given reprieves and that money would have to start coming in in a hurry.

So she accepted the job—and promised herself that she would never be seen on the street in her work clothes. She had bought a used but still very nice leather briefcase online. She put her work clothes in it. Anyone seeing her on the street would think she was carrying a laptop because she had one of the jobs that insiders have.

Every day, she was at least five minutes early—plenty of time to change, out of sight of the outside world, from the insider look to the clichéd outsider look in a job for outsiders, which is what she was now.

Today, more than ever, she was aware of her profession—the cliché she had to live by. There were a lot of mirrors in the house, and every time she stole a glance at herself, she had a painful reminder that she was an outsider and that this job was bringing her no closer to the life of an insider.

That morning, another slew of envelopes had been dropped onto her doormat. They looked pretty much like the one that had appeared the day she'd decided to take this job after all. However, this time the contents were much more serious. Rather than just being doubled, in two cases, the amounts were eight times higher. Even paying in installments would be too much of a monthly expense, given what she was now earning.

This was the first time in a long time that she and her husband had had a real argument. His nights out, on top of all these bills, had sparked a discussion that hadn't been had for months, simply because Maria had given up and accepted that she had to do all the heavy lifting, for the sake of her son and her dream of being an insider.

She had calculated for her husband, on a single sheet of paper, how long it would take, given what was now due, her income, and their current savings, for them to hit rock bottom: five months. It was clear to her that her husband also had no more than five months to generate enough income from somewhere to buy some more time than that for them so she could find a better solution in the meantime.

Her husband told her his honor had been besmirched by what she had written down. The figures themselves, he said, were secondary to the condescension that fairly dripped from the sheet of paper. After a tirade full of sound and fury and marked by an impressive variety of arm flailing, he had torn the page into little shreds. How could she even think of explaining to him, a mathematician, the financial consequences of this situation? He was doing everything he could to change things, and she knew full well, didn't she, that he was working on big things, which simply take time. All really important work took time, he said.

So there she was with her outsider look, in her outsider's job. It was bad enough having to stuff her work clothes into her laptop bag every morning just to get out of the house past this shiftless man, who shiftlessly did not need a wake-up call and shiftlessly snored the building awake every morning. Now that she knew that the work was not enough to sustain this life she did not want, and that no matter what happened she would be bankrupt in five months, it was harder than ever to motivate herself. Whether she came up a little bit or very short each month didn't matter so much— short was short.

She picked up a dustpan and broom. The same set she picked up effortlessly day in, day out seemed to weigh an absolute ton. She started sweeping, and with each movement the broom seemed to get heavier and heavier. After just a few minutes, she felt all out of breath, and dropped the broom and the metal dustpan. Its sharp edge struck the marble floor. That didn't bother her. She didn't care that the marble had been flown in from Italy.

She had a feeling of heaviness in her shoulders and her neck. It was becoming hard to get enough air. She was now gasping for breath.

Everything faded to black.

*        *        *

She opened her eyes and became aware of her surroundings. She recalled vaguely what had happened. She was sitting on the floor, propped up against a white built-in cupboard. Someone had put a damp cloth on her neck, and a little too close to her right foot, there was a glass of water with a flat white pill next to it. There was no one around.

"Hello? Anybody there?" She didn't want to be too loud, but she needn't have worried; her voice wouldn't have been heard even by the best-trained dog. She tried again, a little louder. "Hello? Anyone?"

Nothing. She thought she heard a vacuum cleaner in the distance. It could also have been a fan or the sound of the pump that kept the pool clean, or warm—she'd never been quite clear on which.

She stared ahead. Every second felt like fifteen minutes. She felt she'd been there for hours. She did not move. It even seemed as if she wasn't blinking.

What had become of her? She was so far from the only one, apart from her little boy, that she loved and could ever love at her age. And the dream of being an insider? She was working as an outsider, only to find that she could not afford even *that* life.

She never wanted to admit it, but she'd always looked down on the other outsiders. She thought they made her look bad. She saw herself differently. Yes, she was an outsider now, but at least an outsider who was on her way to having the life of an insider.

Everything had changed now. The pile of envelopes, her husband's yelling, and these last minutes of physical discomfort. It was as if someone had thrown a glass of ice-cold water in her face. While she was recovering from that, a voice echoed in her head, shouting, "Once an outsider, always an outsider! Outsider, outsider, through and through!"

And after all her efforts—moving here, searching for and holding down jobs, and the changes her son had to go through—all it had led to was this.

She'd have to pull herself together.

She'd come such a long way, away from her father. She had taken a leap—and why? For herself and her son. The rest was, and remained, unimportant. She just *had* to have the life of an insider, come what may.

She grabbed onto a protrusion on a bronze sculpture—a small branch in a forest scene with a howling wolf—and pulled herself up. She stood up and took a deep breath—so deep that she then spluttered a cough before being able to take another, shallower breath.

"The insider dream—come what may." The sentence repeated itself in her head at a tempo that seemed to keep exactly with a perfectly timed metronome. Ba-dada-da-DA, da da da.

She just had to do it. Yes, she was an outsider, but only for now. She was different, and smarter. Not book smart, but smart all the same. Intuitively smart, with more stick-to-it-iveness. She was determined to climb out of the abyss, out of this cliché. She had to get away from the cliché. Insiders had all these prejudices, and it was up to her to show them that not all outsiders are outsiders. She had to show them what an outsider could become. But if, at the moment, in the outsider's life she now had, people were determined to see her that way, why not just live the cliché? Making use of the ready-to-hand clichés. Clichés were there for a reason. They also have to be put to the test before they can become clichés. It happens once, and then a second time—and then it stands out. One forms a hypothesis that this new phenomenon could well be a cliché. And only if it continues can it start to be called a cliché.

Maria picked up the glass of water from the ground, leaving the flat white pill where it was. There was a prejudice that immediately came to mind—the cliché that people never say out loud but that you could still hear them saying.

"Oh, you've hired an immigrant. Time to install the security cameras."

"Oh, from Colombia, you say? I'd keep a close eye on my bag if I were you."

She'd heard it all before, without anyone's ever having to say it.

She'd always been annoyed, even irritated, by thieves. Taking away someone else's property was bad enough, but doing it unprofessionally was far worse.

She'd seen boys not much older than her son snatching things. Very unsubtly, they'd head for their mark, often in groups of four or more. You could see it coming. They'd snatch what they were after—which was often worth next to nothing, especially in view of the risk—and immediately head-tail it.

She had never considered stealing, but she had thought about how to do it better. It would have to go undetected and involve only items that were worth many times the risk of being caught. She'd have to make sure she could get rid of it easily, and she would never run with it. It would have to fit in her laptop bag among her work clothes—nothing else for the outside world to see. There was already enough prejudice because of the color of her skin, so there was no need for a suspicious sprint or a large, strangely wrapped object.

She began to clean without thinking. Somehow, she had programmed herself to think of one thing, often related to her long-term insider dream, even as she busied herself with the here and now. In fact, she found that she seemed to be working faster than usual in order to make up for the time she'd lost.

As she began to mop the ground, she thought about her big move toward insider-ship. In the meantime, she had taught herself that stealing did not necessarily have to be what the clichéd outsider did.

If she were to steal in style, it could fall outside stereotypes. She had seen an American film with a handsome elderly man. He had become such a master criminal that everyone saw him as a hero within five minutes, even as he spent his time preparing and carrying out one bank robbery after another.

That's how she would also behave. The goal would be the same. Making other people's things your own. However, she would do it like Robin Hood. Stealing from those who did not need it. And she would do it in a certain way. It's how you did it that was key. She would come up with a method with minimum risk and maximum returns relative to that risk.

She even started humming an old Colombian tune. That was always a good sign for her. The sun began to shine, and the memory of the pile of mail that morning began to fade.

She looked around. What would her first move be? She knew how to find many beautiful things without much of an effort. Silver cutlery—probably worth a lot and easy to transport, but where would she to put it? The electronics from the media room? Something small that looked very precious and that everyone was browsing for online? Or the antique books in the library? Not far from her bus stop, there was a shop that bought and sold that kind of stuff. She was always surprised by the prices in the window.

She told herself she didn't have to think about the objects and the proceeds immediately. That was what normal thieves did, not the amiable master criminal she would have to be—just for a time, because as soon as she could be done being a criminal and start living the insider life, she'd have made it.

She first had to figure out how to grab something without anyone's noticing or missing it immediately or being able to see it, either from afar or from, say, a camera—and she hadn't seen a single one of those anywhere in the ridiculously large home.

She paused a moment. Slowly, her thoughts moved from room to room. By now, she knew the place like the back of her hand—every nook and cranny. She thought of places that people came to the least. There were places where no one would look or notice. Better still, where there could be small, precious objects, without anyone's finding it odd that they should be there.

One of the pantries? No, an expensive item would stand out too much. In one of the lockers in the private gym? No, why would anyone—never mind the owner—put any small expensive item in a gym locker? One of the toilets—nope. Walk-in closets—no way.

The hobby room.

Yes—the hobby room above the garage. That place was perfect. There were all sorts of things lying around there. Every time she was there, she noticed. There were so many different types of objects. Some were unscrewed, some were half-unpacked, and a lot of them were just lying around.

The more she thought about this spot, the stronger it seemed as a candidate. And she knew that Mr. David hadn't used the garage or the space above it in recent months. She'd already come across the garage and the room above it several times in her cleaning rounds. She'd noticed that the cars had not been used and that everything was in the same place in the hobby room. The owner didn't really come out of the main house anymore. Better still, he used only a very small part, perhaps only four of the countless rooms at his disposal.

She walked to the schedule for all the staff in the main room. Behind her, there were still a lot of mugs on the table, quite a few still with tea or coffee in them. She briefly recalled that she had woken up with water and a pill beside her. Someone had put them here. Someone had helped her. Had they discussed this at length here?

It didn't matter. She quickly shifted her attention back to the schedule.

She moved her finger down the list until she found today's date. A quick look to the right—three days to go before she had to do the garage. *Perfect,* she thought. That gave her several days to look for small objects. Items no one would miss. It also gave her enough time to think about where to sell the items. Tonight, she could look on the internet to see which products were in high demand. She also thought she should do everything in cash. She'd have to meet buyers in person. If she did anything through the bank, it would be too conspicuous.

She would move objects of interest from one place to another in the house before removing them so she could sell them. *Watertight,* she thought. No one would notice. And if someone were to look for the objects in the hobby room, they could still find them. Better yet, if anyone *were* to notice something, they would just put it back. Wherever "back" was. No one would declare the object stolen. It would just go back to the place where it always lay, unused. And then step two, after she'd made sure no one had noticed, would be to remove it from the house and sell it.

Watertight. She would see that evening which bills she could settle with cash. And she would search the internet and the neighborhood for what was in demand.

A master criminal. She had never thought about it like that. Would her father be proud of her? His daughter would not be a thief but a master criminal. As long as she stopped as soon as she had achieved her dream of being an insider.

# 9. DAVID

David was startled awake.

He remembered the years when an alarm clock would wake him every morning, but this was worse. Many times worse.

He woke up in complete silence. The sun had clearly been up for some time, and in the distance, he could hear a vacuum cleaner humming away in a part of his house where he would probably not be for the next few weeks.

He rubbed his eyes, searched for his trusty lip balm, and grabbed his phone.

"Dad's lecture club."

David felt his heart beat ten times faster in his chest. He was standing next to his bed within seconds.

He started the shower with his app and quickly squeezed some toothpaste onto a toothbrush. He shortened his shower time from twenty minutes to half a minute and clumsily shaved off just a little too much of his sideburns.

There was little in his life that David loved less than fashion. Nevertheless, several cupboards were filled with all kinds of recently purchased clothes—mostly informal, casual items. David hated buying clothes and had resolved years before never to go into a clothing shop again. His tactic was simple: every time an advertisement appeared on his phone for an item of clothing that met three criteria, he bought it. The criteria: it was on offer, it looked all right, and it was available in his size. The idea was that he would then not need last-minute clothes. Hypothetically, having to do that could entail going to a brick-and-mortar shop. He had thought long and hard about whether the criterion that an item had to be on offer made any sense, given his financial situation, but he had stuck to it, simply because he did not want to let the sector have the full margin.

After a good long search, he found an outfit that he considered formal enough for his father's event. He found a button-down shirt—a garment he hoped he'd never have to wear again starting from this point in his life.

He also disliked the leather shoes and the neat trousers. However, he thought to himself time and time again that wearing them was well worth it if it meant he wouldn't have to put up with the comments and dour expressions from his father and his friends.

He called for a taxi and immediately ordered breakfast, which would have to arrive five minutes before the taxi.

While waiting, he thought, just in time, that his dad would send him some ideas for what to say. Actually, his story had been ready for a long time. He had talked all about his "rise to fame" several times, in several languages, over the last few months. "A classic tale of rags to riches" is what the Americans had called it, not knowing that he did not exactly come from "rags." He understood that it served the purposes of the story—and who was he to make a beautiful story less entertaining by telling the truth?

He had not looked at his personal email for quite some time. A bunch of fortune-seekers with "no-risk" investments of all kinds. He did not know what made him more uncomfortable: investments "without risk" or prospectuses that explicitly stated that they involved a lot of risk. In recent years, he had put most of his money into really boring asset management options that offered the lowest possible costs and that didn't require that he have a lot of human contact. For example, there was a start-up where he suspected he had provided more than half of the equity they invested "most conservatively," according to their app. They had called him to thank him for his trust, and he had indicated as subtly as he could that the best way to thank him was to stop calling him. "Just take care of my money," he had said two or three times.

He immediately saw an email from his father in his inbox. Of all the names in his list of contacts, this was the only that was preceded by an academic title.

He opened the email, titled "Pointers for the Lecture at the Club." Below that, there was a remark in italics: "It would be nice if you could incorporate the points below—obviously only if they fit in with your story."

He quickly scanned the text underneath. It was quite amazing how much his father had typed. It was as if he had devoted an entire novel to points that David might possibly incorporate into his story, which he had just a few minutes to tell.

He quickly switched to another app on his phone and sent a message to his father. The thought of him nervously sitting at his table in the midst of all his friends made him uneasy, but secretly he also enjoyed it a little.

"Father, I'm almost there. Incompetent driver."

This excuse had the best chance of succeeding. He was sure that the suboptimal performance of the workforce that included a taxi driver would give his father at the club enough ammunition to make his tardiness tolerable. David thought about how everyone would nod in understanding at the message and take turns sharing their worst experiences with drivers in their past.

He switched back to his father's notes.

". . . just like that one time—I think you were just eight. You wanted to give up, but I taught you to persevere . . . You were about to go off the beaten track, but I helped you see that you could do more. You have entrepreneurship in your blood, just like my father and me . . ."

His reading was interrupted by the arrival of the driver, who was perfectly on time. David asked the driver to wait a moment because his breakfast was late. He had just seen a message on the app he'd ordered through, BreakFAST: "Your order has just left our kitchen!" *So much for THAT name*, he thought. The driver agreed after David promised him a nice tip.

Fortunately, breakfast actually wasn't long in arriving. It would have been unfair not to give the delivery guy a tip since part of his drive had been along David's driveway and since it wasn't his fault the kitchen had been late. David selected "15 percent" from among the options, even as he wondered whether the delivery guy himself would actually get that amount.

David quickly got into the taxi. Under one arm was the breakfast that had just been delivered: bircher muesli and a croissant with Emmentaler cheese and Spanish ham. Under the other, there were a few sheets of paper and in his mouth, a blue plastic ballpoint. For years, David had gotten all kinds of comments about the way he used his pen. Some found it incomprehensible that a digital entrepreneur still used pen and paper. He himself found it quite understandable. He found it even more incomprehensible that some people found it odd that he still wrote with the simplest available blue ballpoint pens. The way they saw it, he had to write with pens on which his name was engraved. Pens that you pick up, not from a transparent plastic tray holding a lot of similar pens but from a specially designed pen holder containing pens that have been ergonomically optimized by generations of Swiss specialists—men and women who have dedicated their lives to finding the best way to get thoughts from brain to hand, to pen, to paper.

The more marketing blah-blah he heard, the more he longed for even simpler pens. He used a pen for as long as possible, until it was so worn out that he would get ink in his mouth whenever he held it between his teeth while thinking or typing a message. Only then would he think about getting a new one—the simplest one he could find.

In the taxi, David balanced a piece of paper on his left knee, holding it in place with his left elbow even as he ate his croissant with his left hand. With his right, he tried to jot down a few pointers as legibly as possible—little reminders here and there that should give his father something to brag about.

It was clear to David. This lecture was his way of giving back. He would pay his father back for the times he'd been there for him and for the financial support he'd given him. He was aware that he had never expected that much from his father. He was no psychologist, but it was clear to him that he should have been able to expect his father would be around more, to show him more love and give him more encouragement. Yet, as he had to keep reminding himself, one of the reasons his father had been away so much was to pay for his upkeep. So this was his way of repaying him. In a way, it was even selfish; he was doing this in the same way he bought clothes. He bought clothes not because he needed new clothes now, but just so he wouldn't have to buy them later. In the same way, he was doing this now so he wouldn't have to feel guilty later on or try to come up with a real way to repay the people who had brought him into the world and kept him alive in his early years.

He now had a few simple bullet points on his sheet of paper.

- Give him credit for entrepreneurial character

- Emphasize perseverance—inherited from Dad

He heard the taxi driver ask something. The dialect was hard to pin down.

"Sorry, what was that?"

"Are you making a drawing?"

"Ha ha, no—just jotting down a few notes. I have to deliver a few remarks."

"Are you a minister or something?"

"A minister? Ha ha, no, I would be the most unsuitable minister ever."

The driver didn't answer. David did not know whether he'd offended him by laughing at his question about being a minister. He felt pressure to respect the man and explain who he was. Preferably something close to a minister so that the good man would not think he was ridiculing him. But he didn't want to overdo it, either.

"No, I once built a business. I'll be talking to a group of people who want to know what that was like and what I learned from it."

"Oh, OK, so you're an entrepreneur."

David noticed he had not expected the driver to use the word "entrepreneur." He was ashamed of the prejudice he harbored that someone who spoke in this dialect and who looked like the driver did would not have this word in his vocabulary. He made a mental note to try to get rid of this kind of prejudice. Unfortunately, he'd already had to say this to himself several times, but that hadn't done the trick yet. There were few people he looked down on, but he simply couldn't stand racists and an arrogant aristocracy.

"Yes, sir." David said "sir" to make up for the thoughts he was having.

"What kind of business did you have? Dry cleaning? Or something with boats? I saw someone on television the other day who had made a lot of money with boats."

"No, neither of those. I had some restaurants."

"Restaurants? There must have been quite a lot of them for you to own a house like that."

"Yes, quite a few." David didn't want to say how many. Mentioning the number of RoboWok outlets there were when he sold the business would have come across as boastful, and there was no need to say how many in this casual back and forth.

"Must have been really pricey places, with lobster and stuff."

"Ha ha, no. The opposite, in fact. We were selling the cheapest full meal in many places."

"What do you mean by "full meal'?"

David didn't know why he'd felt the need to say anything other than "cheap meal." Now he had given away more than he'd needed to for a trip like this.

"With us, you got everything you needed at a very low price."

"You mean vegetables, meat, and so on."

"Yes, exactly. For the same money, you could get a hamburger or some tacos elsewhere. But with us, you got more than your daily allowance of vegetables, protein, basically all the building blocks you need for a healthy life."

"That's the kind of stuff I should be eating." He smiled as he gave his belly a few loud slaps.

"Oh well, you have to enjoy life a little bit too, right?" He was trying not to come off as pompous. He did not want to show that he was paying attention to his diet and thus considered himself superior. Of course, everyone had the right to weigh health against the enjoyment of a hamburger or an ice cream after dinner.

"Are the restaurants themselves still around? Maybe it will be nice for my wife when this boy gets a bit smaller." The driver slapped his belly again but more gently this time. Then he squeezed the roll of fat just below his navel.

"Yeah, there are still a few here and there." David quickly tried to think of a way to point the man to a location without making it clear that he had been the owner of the fastest-growing restaurant chain there had been in recent years.

"There's one in the village on the left here." David pointed through the closed window of the taxi. He knew that by now he could point to just about any inhabited area and there'd be a good chance it had a RoboWok.

"On the main street, you can find a counter, often where there used to be an ATM or maybe a vending machine."

"What is it called?"

"RoboWok."

David saw the driver looking very unsubtly in his rearview mirror. In his eyes, he saw something that looked like terror. He felt the driver thinking, *I have that guy from RoboWok, right here, in my taxi.*

"Oh, here we are." David was really happy that the destination was so close. He wanted nothing more than to stop this conversation. Chances were that he would've had to talk about the growth of RoboWok—how he had come up with it and all the rest. He would have been perfectly happy to do that, except that he'd be telling the story again at his dad's club in just a few minutes.

"Nice to meet you—and thanks for the great service. It's worth a good tip."

"Well I certainly hope so, Mr. RoboWok Big Shot," the driver answered with a mischievous smile. David imagined the good man worked the same long hours day in, day out but that his pay was always linear. Or perhaps there was even a negative correlation between the number of hours he worked and what he took in as an hourly average. The taxi platform probably allocated incremental rides with a pricing algorithm that worked to his detriment. In his view, David had lucked out, so he might as well share some of his good fortune with the hardworking man.

However, David didn't want to tip him too much. It was perhaps a bad principle of his, but he had certain rules he lived by. A tip was always going to be a certain percentage of the amount due, regardless of his wealth. He didn't want to reward the driver for his good fortune. It was pure luck that he had David as a customer and that a few minutes earlier he'd had to wait extra for David's breakfast to arrive, so he would get an unreasonably greater reward than if he'd had some other customer who was waiting for a taxi at the same time. David thought it was unfair to all the other drivers and that there should be a reasonable ratio between the quality of the service given and the amount of pay received.

He was approached before he was ready for it by a man who was too well dressed for the role he was playing. He did not hear the first part of what he said because he was still too busy calibrating the amount of the driver's tip.

". . . and thank you for coming. It's such a bother that the driver could not provide a timely service. May I take your coat?"

David felt embarrassed at what he'd said about the driver. He had kept the good man waiting, and now everyone in his father's club thought his service wasn't up to par.

"Would you like something before you start? A glass of water, perhaps, or an espresso? Or maybe a peppermint?"

David found it odd to be offered a peppermint. Did he have bad breath? However, he would be standing on a podium and speaking from a good distance, so even if he did, it wouldn't matter.

"A glass of water, at room temperature, please."

"Certainly, sir. This way, please."

David was led by the well-dressed man to a small room next to the main hall. From the main hall, he heard a strange mix of low voices in heated discussion and others roaring with laughter.

"You can relax here a few moments and gather your thoughts while I get your water. What time shall I announce you?"

"In five minutes?" David regretted that he had answered so quickly; a quarter of an hour would have been fine and would not have been too much.

"As you wish, sir. Break a leg."

"Thanks." David found the phrase a bit odd here, but perhaps this is what they usually said before a talk.

"The taxi sector let him down, but he is now here. Thank you all for your kind patience. And now, ladies and gentlemen, it is my pleasure to invite to the podium Mr. RoboWok himself."

There was polite applause—nothing compared to the clapping and cheering he had sometimes experienced in much larger venues. Not long ago, he had spoken in front of a few hundred students. On his arrival there, a large group had chanted "Ro-bo-Wok! Ro-bo-Wok!"

David tried adjusting the microphone a bit, but it didn't move easily, so he decided to take it out of its holder. He looked around the room and soon saw his father, which made him grow unexpectedly emotional. It was only now he realized that his father had grown much older in a short time. There he was, with his thumbs up, looking at his son.

David began his story. The same story he had told so many times before. How he envisaged a future where people could experience the convenience of not cooking for themselves at a price that was accessible to everyone but not at the expense of quality. How, unlike his competitors, he needed far fewer square miles for his branches and how the fixed costs of labor accounted for a much smaller part of his profits and losses.

Fortunately, halfway through the second half of his story, he quickly looked at his notes.

In a slightly forced way, he made it clear that his father's perseverance had helped him through difficult times and that entrepreneurship ran in his blood. He took a quick look at his father out of the corner of his eye to gauge his reaction. He saw how he looked around, looking for eye contact with his peers and getting pats on the back.

There was no natural ending to David's story. He hadn't added a nice twist at the end or any edifying moral, even though he had given many versions of it. He just stopped.

David filled the silence that suddenly permeated the room. "Are there any questions?"

It was quiet for a moment. Then, just as though they were in a classroom, he saw a man, who was wearing glasses that were very small for the size of his head, raise his hand.

"Yes, sir?"

"Thanks for the great story, young man— very inspiring. I recognized a lot of it. Quite a few parts reminded me of the hurdles I faced during my career."

"You were also an entrepreneur?"

"Something of the sort. I was in charge of the largest business unit of a logistics company."

David's father had done exactly the same thing—pretended to have overcome the same hurdles when in fact he'd had a steady job with a major corporation.

"Aha, I see. And what question do you have for me today?"

"Well, young man. You have not said much about life after the acquisition. What is it that keeps you busy now? What are you investing in? How are you enjoying the wealth you've acquired?"

"Well . . ." David could not think of a less interesting question. "I have built a house, and every now and then I tell my story. Next question please."

In the back, a slightly smaller but even better dressed man started talking unannounced. It was unclear whether it was an introduction to a question.

"After toiling for so many years, the transition is challenging. I remember well when I stepped down as CEO. There were, of course, still advisory boards, but ..."

David soon lost focus. It was a risk, because the story of the well-dressed man could lead to a question at any moment. He decided that he would resolve it when the time came. He looked at his father again, who was sitting in a posture that was unusual for a man of his age. His legs were sticking out in front, toward the stage, and almost all of his upper body was arched backward as he spoke to the men at the table behind him. He saw the men laughing at his story. It was actually a little bit rude, David thought. They were making a lot of noise while this man was in the middle of a story. A story that could have a question tagged onto it at any moment.

"... don't you think?"

David was startled out of his own thoughts. "Apologies, I didn't catch the last part."

"I understand. The noise doesn't help." The man looked sternly toward the table behind his father. That table immediately fell silent. It was clear that this man was somewhere at the top of the internal pecking order.

"Do you also feel pressure to engage in philanthropy?"

"Yes. You have to share what is given to you, of course."

"Exactly, but you have to entertain yourself at the same time, don't you?"

The audience found the man's remark very funny. David didn't understand why. There was almost half a minute of laughter, and in another corner, he saw people mimicking golf swings and lighting make-believe cigars. When things calmed down a bit, David took his chance.

"Thank you so much for your kind attention. It was an honor to speak to you here. Please excuse me. I must be off. You know how it is."

David was very happy with his last sentence. He knew that the group of old white men all wanted to show their peers that they were still very busy, even though they had all retired long ago. Everyone would "know how it is" or would at least want to make it seem as though they did.

"We understand."

"Nailed it. Well done," David said to himself. He managed to hide his smile just in time.

"Gentlemen, are there any urgent questions, or can the kitchen start on the next course?"

It was unclear who had asked this question. But the male voice had enough authority to make the whole room listen and agree.

"One last question." Close to the stage sat a smaller man, who did not try to compensate for his height with exclusive clothing.

"What do you want to be in ten years?"

It was the first meaningful question David had had. He was a bit taken aback, but also pleased. Finally, a question about something other than his recently acquired wealth and not about the things he had bought or would buy. At the same time, the question was a bit too heavy for this occasion. Subconsciously, he had been thinking about it—perhaps about little else, in fact. He didn't have an answer yet, and he didn't feel that this was the time to force one out. He looked around the room, and his first internal response was that he didn't want to end up like these guys. He stopped himself before he could express that thought—that would be gratuitously unkind. He would just leave them be. "Be jealous that they've found what they were looking for in this place," he told himself.

"I'm considering a number of options," he lied.

"Interesting. Can you give us a hint?"

"I'm afraid I'll have to take a rain check on that one. Sorry."

For a moment, David was afraid that this would lead to a new invitation. He quickly left the stage. Behind him, he heard the same unfamiliar voice go through the program for the following week.

He headed for the exit. The man who had been waiting for him earlier came after him with his coat.

"Oh, thank you. I almost forgot."

"You must have many other coats at home. Thank you for coming."

# 10. BERNARD

"The apple doesn't fall far from the tree, old chap."

"Ah yes, that is what they say." Bernard tried to respond as humbly as he could. He had been showered with compliments for the last twenty, perhaps thirty, minutes. At one point, even the treasurer had come to him to tell him how inspiring he had found the story and added that more fathers should prepare their sons for such a path. "And such self-confidence. To hold your own in front of such an audience. Telling your story like that, as if you were talking to a group of bakers in a village somewhere in the middle of the country."

"I told him emphatically, 'Tell your story the way you always do. Don't make any adjustments purely to suit the audience.'"

Bernard had made a big point of this in the notes he had sent David. He knew that his son would never read the whole document, so he had underlined this part and marked it with exclamation marks at several points.

"Interesting how entrepreneurship is a nature thing, not exactly nurture."

"I've always been surprised by that too, Gerard. Funny you should say that. I used to be much more enterprising than the rest, just like my own father."

"The apple doesn't fall far from the tree." This was, Bernard thought, the twentieth time that someone had said exactly that to him.

He stood up, fastened the right number of buttons on his jacket, and walked toward the restroom. Not the toilet—the restroom. "We don't say 'toilet,'" Bernard had always said at least once a week to his family.

He tried to find the right pace as he made his way to the restroom. Not too fast so that he could still receive a few pats on the back here and there, but certainly not too slow either. His body was still surprisingly fit for his age, but he had to listen carefully to his bladder and not keep it waiting. He would not want to ruin this moment.

"Excellently done!"

"What a beautiful specimen that boy of yours is!"

"Bravo, Bernard. Let's catch up soon. Dinner's on me."

He couldn't get enough of it, but he really had to listen to his bladder. On the second leg toward the restroom, he accelerated, only to arrive at the urinal slightly out of breath. He did not yet have an opinion on the word urinal, or an alternative.

He urinated with a healthy jet exactly in the direction of the little fly that was painted on the ceramic. When everything was under control, he looked up. There were round mirrors on the wall at eye level. "Eye level" was taken quite literally. That's exactly what Bernard could see: his eyes but not the rest of his face.

He looked at himself. If the room went dark, he would probably still be able to see himself. It was as if his eyes and his forehead were glowing. His head seemed to be radioactive, positively glowing with pride. He had not known many moments like this in his life. Yes, he was a successful man. That much was obvious from his house, his cars, his hobbies, and his attire. But his success had come from being obedient enough every day at work—from doing what was asked of him. This moment had not come "from above." Nobody had told him to have a child. Nobody had told his son to use his genes to produce such a magical thing. It was a self-made peak of happiness, instead of the much smaller peaks he had always felt. He had had good days: a compliment from the boss, good monthly figures, a happy customer, an unexpectedly high bonus. He had sung along with a record on the radio in the car afterward. Something he would never let his friends know. This peak, however, this feeling of pride, of having really achieved something, was quite different.

Bernard washed his hands and combed the hair he still had left with a small comb he always carried in his inside pocket. He looked down at his trousers and a little farther down at his shoes. He wondered whether he was properly dressed for the occasion.

He left the restroom and almost bumped into the cloakroom attendant.

"Apologies, sir."

"No problem, young man. I was the one who almost bumped into you."

"Yes, but I might have chosen a better place."

"You're right about that. Let it be a lesson. By the way, have you seen my son?"

"Your son, sir?"

"Today's speaker. A younger gentleman than you're used to seeing." Bernard found himself very charming and was pleased with his choice of words.

"Ah yes, he came to me for his coat right after his speech. So you must be 'Big Daddy RoboWok.'"

"Now let's not get too chummy, young fellow." Bernard had his limits. He noticed that he was responding in this way because he was disappointed that his son had left in such a hurry.

"I'm sorry, sir." The young man took a step back and bowed his head.

"No, *my* apologies. Yes, I am 'Big Daddy RoboWok.' A proud father."

"I understand that, sir. It's quite something that your son has achieved."

"We are very proud of it indeed. The apple doesn't fall . . ."

". . . far from the tree, sir?"

"That's it indeed."

Bernard took a mint from the bowl next to the attendant. He put a quarter for him on the tray next to it, thinking this was a nice tidy sum on top of his salary.

He then turned around to walk toward the hall. He faltered. The glowing feeling he had had in the restroom suddenly disappeared. He turned back in the other direction, toward the front door.

"Could you please get me my coat, too?"

"But of course, sir."

It was unclear to Bernard how the system worked. He had not given the attendant a number. There was no hook with his name on it, and the attendant didn't know his name, even though he could now guess since he knew that he was "Big Daddy RoboWok." Yet within half a minute, he had his coat on. The boy had deftly helped him with it, so all he had to do was zip it up.

"I'm going to get some air. All that sitting inside does no good."

"Sounds like a good idea. Would you like an umbrella, sir? There's a slight drizzle."

"No thanks." Bernard knew few words that made his toes curl the way "drizzle" did.

Once outside, Bernard decided to walk toward the entry to the estate. He had come by car, but he needed the air. And he did not live very far from the club. Not what one would call walking distance, but walkable with the right mindset.

How could he go from euphoria to this feeling so quickly? He had perhaps never felt such euphoria. Not even when David was born, not at his wedding, and not when he had received his master's degree.

His son had become his greatest work, his *magnum opus*. He had brought him into the world and made sure that he was ready to stand on his own feet when he came of age. He had taken him on holiday and had told him how much he liked his drawing, even though there were just a few random lines on the paper.

Bernard decided not to think about anything and just keep walking. Not thinking about anything was an impossible task, though. So he tried to shift his thoughts to purely practical matters. The house had to be repainted, and he was already thinking about the next holiday he had to book. Fortunately, the rain was quite light. It was damp, but the moisture on his face made the length of the walk more bearable. It had been a long time since he had traveled such a distance without the help of fossil fuels.

He had arrived at a junction where he had been hundreds of times before by car. This was the first time he had come across it on foot. *Funny,* he thought, *that road signs are so much bigger in real life than they seem when you see them from the car.* Every time he'd stood here before—the light had always seemed to turn red just as he was approaching—he'd looked at the thatched cottage on the other side of the intersection. He had always turned left, toward home. He had never gone straight ahead and never turned in the direction of the thatched cottage.

On the gable end, just below the highest point of the thatch, a German-sounding brand of beer was showing on an illuminated display, thus indicating that this place was open to the public. He could go in and buy a drink. It was one of those days, a day for new experiences. A day to not turn left for once.

He crossed over, even though it seemed that there was no footpath. The road he was on was meant only for cars. Fortunately, there were no cars to be seen in the distance.

He started up the path toward the bistro. It was clearly not "just a pub" because daily specials were advertised on a chalkboard. He walked toward the front door. He turned the doorknob, but just as he was about to push the door open, in the corner of his eye he saw his son, David.

For a moment he considered knocking on the window. But he didn't. That would have been quite out of character for him. Besides, it would be more fun if he surprised his son by suddenly standing behind him.

Bernard stood still, his son's face preventing him from walking on. There he sat, the boy—no, a man now—who had made him feel the greatest euphoria he'd ever felt in his life.

David's face, however, showed something quite different from euphoria. He had a cup of tea in front of him. Or rather hot water with all kinds of fresh herbs in it. He was looking straight ahead, the index finger of his right hand slowly tracing the top of the tea glass in small circles.

His gaze was quite vacant. It seemed that, except for the finger on the tea glass, his whole body was absolutely still. That he was not even blinking. A blank, glazed-over look. He had not taken off his coat, even though it looked nice and warm in the restaurant.

Bernard took a step to the right, farther from the window. He did not know whether he wanted to be seen, nor whether David did, for that matter.

# 11. NATASHA

Natasha always thought that time flew only when life was entertaining. The last six weeks had flown by, even though each day, each hour, each minute, it had seemed that time was at a standstill.

They had asked for pretty much all processes to be mapped out. Who did what, how often, and in what order. Whether something thing happened once in a certain way or at some regular interval. What the back-up procedure was if something went wrong.

Everyone knew that there were simply no formal processes. If David had done anything right—aside from starting the most valuable business anyone had seen in the last few years—it was that, for the most part, he'd hired self-starters. Natasha had never had a colleague ask her for process statements. People started, took on the area or the deliverable they were responsible for, and just did their own thing.

And now here she was, staring at a stack of documents in binders. One of the new people had even designed a special front cover. *Well* that *must have been a very fruitful use of their time,* she thought. There were dozens of pages of schematic drawings. Each process was fleshed out with whos, whats, and whens and with arrows denoting fixed scenarios and footnotes for exceptions. It had required the mindset of a monk in a lonely tower, even though there was nothing in the least monkish about Natasha's lifestyle.

She was neither happy with nor proud of the end result. She'd found it a waste of time, both while she was doing it and when she'd finished. Worse yet, she strongly suspected that it would never see the light of day, or if not *never,* then perhaps briefly before being buried away somewhere in a filing cabinet in a dark and dank basement archive at head office.

The only positive thing that came out of the whole exercise, Natasha began to see, was that it forced her to reflect on her time on this earth. This kind of work was precisely what she did not want to be doing—working herself to the bone on a deliverable that, given what it was worth, should have taken a few seconds but ended up taking six weeks. Natasha had done a calculation: The average life expectancy for women was 83.3 years. She was just over a quarter of the way there. This meant that she still had about fifty-five years to go. Assuming that she used fifteen years of that time just being old, she landed on the number forty. Forty years to go on this earth, in this form. That was 14,610 days on Earth, including leap years once every four years. That was over 2,087 weeks and a few days. The last six weeks had felt like a day. This meant that, intuitively, if she continued like this, she would have just under 348 days to go.

This was the existential question that a lot of people would not face until much later in life. But she'd run up against it because of the situation—her role in the new version of her company—like a bright yellow Ferrari that had not seen the brick wall up ahead. Even though Natasha was not one to call herself a Ferrari, she hoped, or had hoped, that people would have that kind of impression of her later on.

How many of the intuitively calculated 348 days that she had left on this Earth was Natasha going to spend on process mapping? More to the point: How many of those days was she going to spend doing things that mattered? And an even tougher question: What were the things that mattered?

On week five, she had already subtly indicated to her new boss—the word "boss" had never felt so inappropriate—that this was not the job she'd hoped to be doing over the next few years in her role. She had tried to do it as subtly as possible, striking a balance between being a pleaser and being an empowered woman in charge of her own destiny.

Her new boss was clearly still intimidated by his new role. He was in the phase after the one in which he was happy with the new title and probably the higher pay that went with it. The scope of the role and what he had to deliver, though, now clearly scared him, even though he tried to appear cool and collected.

He had not given much of an answer to Natasha's subtle question about the future interpretation of her role. He clearly thought he had better things to do. He'd said that this was temporary—a "necessary evil" that would be followed by what he'd called much "sexier" work. He'd added that the work she was doing was very important and that it had to be done for the future of the company. That had been just enough for Natasha to finish it, despite the heavy going in the last stretch.

She had gone to work in good spirits that morning. She had delivered in six weeks what had to be delivered. There was a little bit of pride hidden somewhere in her Calvinism.

She had delivered, and karma, or whatever it was, should now reward her with a nice task. After the past six weeks, she could handle anything as long as the work she was given was worthwhile.

He was not on time. She had been waiting alone in the meeting room for over a quarter of an hour. She was the only one there, with a second cup of coffee that had gone cold and a pile of worthless paper. That did give her a chance to look around the new meeting room. The new owner had promised to preserve the start-up culture and use that energy for future growth. The interior designer had clearly been given this in her brief, and it had resulted in a very hip-looking environment. Vertical gardens, pots of water containing fresh ginger and mint, and, above all, lots of one-liners on every wall: "Do what you love," "Get shit done," and all kinds of other well-intentioned but empty slogans.

It was funny how corporate thought about start-ups. From what she had seen, this kind of interior would have been completely out of place in a real start-up. She had always appreciated that the money was spent on what was best for Robo-Wok, not on accessories for meeting rooms. They had rustled up second-hand tables, all in different shades of white. There were no printers. Printing was just not the done thing. If you really had to print, you were at the mercy of a print shop. The higher price per print was enough to stop people from printing things needlessly. The coffee machine was the only real luxury investment, and it had just been replaced by a soulless machine that dispensed soulless coffee.

And finally, he showed up. He had clearly put his newfound affluence into a wardrobe that, for someone with his title, was clichéd. From top to bottom, it looked perfect—not a thing out of place. He looked for all the world as though he had stepped out of an advertisement. But in this outfit, he couldn't hide the fact that he did not have the body of a model, and his face did not match the beautiful suit at all.

He had clearly had a much longer morning than Natasha. He had large bags under his eyes, and it seemed from the look in them that a large part of his soul had left him.

He came in in a hurry and, as soon as he opened the door, a slew of documents he'd been holding under his arm fell from his grasp.

"Natasha. Good morning," he said.

"Good m—Oh dear! Can I help?"

"No, no, I can manage." As he picked up the documents, he looked uncomfortable. These Italian trousers were clearly not made for crouching in a hurry.

"I made coffee for you, but it's cold now. Would you like a fresh one?" Natasha was trying again to let him know subtly that she'd been waiting a long time, while also being a pleaser.

He didn't apologize but started right in on what he wanted to talk about for the next few minutes. It was clear he didn't want it to take much longer than that.

"This is really good work." He half-stroked, half-patted the pile of processes.

"Are you going to present that to the board?"

"They will be told they've been completed, and they will thus be aware that they're available to them as soon as they're needed. And with your name on them."

"That's nice." Natasha knew that this would never happen. The documents would never see the light of day and would end up in an archive at some global headquarters. Perhaps thousands of years from now, archaeologists would come across the document after years of digging. They would marvel at this "Natasha" from ancient history. Natasha resolved to put this behind her. She had been working on it mentally all weekend, saying to herself over and over again, "The work had to be done, and now it *is* done. Time to focus on the future. The future will be beautiful. The future will make it all worthwhile."

"RoboWok needs people like you. This had to be done, and it *has* been done. And all because of you."

"You're welcome." Natasha was shocked at herself. This was a risk. She was giving him the opportunity to dump more work of this kind on her desk.

"I have great expectations for your future with us. If you keep doing this kind of work, you can expect a lot."

The compliment and this golden future were nice, but Natasha had a strange gut feeling. It felt like he was preparing the ground for more of the same thing. And she had been promised the world before, only to have to go through six weeks of pure and utter misery.

"We have to add time to it. Actually, time and costs."

"To what?"

"Your processes, of course."

"Oh, I see." She'd officially become the "Process Specialist."

"This work will be key to boosting the company's productivity. More value per fixed cost. More value means more investment. More investment in the consumer. A better experience. More shareholder value. Thanks again. Great work!"

Natasha paused for a moment and collected her thoughts. She looked at her options but decided that this was the moment. She had to stand up for herself. She had to make the most of the 348 days she had left on this earth by doing what she found worthwhile.

"Thank you. However . . ."

"Oh—yes?" There was a long silence.

"As I recall, we had said that after this 'necessary evil' I would be able to do what you called 'sexier' work." She made a point of using his words.

"But it doesn't get much sexier than this, does it? This work may lead to major decisions. You are the architect of the incremental value we produce post-acquisition!"

"Oh?" Natasha had no idea what he had just said.

"Your work is going to tell management exactly where we can extract value!"

This further sentence didn't make his message much clearer. "Well, I suppose if you look at it that way." Natasha was disappointed once again by how quickly she had responded. She should have pressed her case further right then and there. Once again, the pleaser had won out over the empowered woman.

"Very nice. Another six weeks seems to me to be a nice deadline again, right? RoboWok is counting on you!"

Her manager rushed out of the room. Without wanting to, Natasha found herself staring at his behind as he left. She thought about selling tickets to a sweepstakes she would organize. Participants could guess when he would burst the seams of his pants. There would be big prizes to be won.

Natasha tried to catch her breath. But before she knew it, he was back. For a moment, she hoped he had had some new insights and had perhaps changed his mind. Maybe he had come back to ask her to do something valuable for a change.

"Before I forget. You really have to fill out the survey this morning. You're on the blacklist."

"Blacklist?"

"You got the link a few weeks ago, didn't you?"

Natasha knew what it was about but decided to pretend it had escaped her.

"Can you forward it again please?"

"Of course. No problem. I understand. Your thoughts were elsewhere. I will send it right away, but please make sure to fill it in this time. This survey shows us whether everyone is really on board with us as we strike out in this new direction. It has to be a common dream!"

Natasha gave a thumbs up, and somewhere in her brain, she randomly decided to respond in Italian. "Pronto."

# 12. BERNARD AND DAVID

“**I** have great news for you, my boy!”

David said nothing and waited for the news.

“Aren't you keen to know what it is?”

David put his hand over his cellphone halfway through a deep sigh—just in time.

“Of course I am, but how can you surprise someone who already has everything?”

“Oh now! Having all the things you want isn't the same as having everything. There's so much more to aspire to. Financial independence is nice, but there's so much more.”

“Such as?”

“Well, how about recognition?”

“From whom, though?”

“Authorities. Authorities that have clout.”

“Clout? White men giving other white men the right to decide, by putting their John

Hancock on a charter with a fancy quill, what someone else can and can't do?"

"That's not it at all, my boy. Not in the least."

"Well . . . my apologies then." David regretted right away that he had apologized. He had to learn not to do that. He'd meant what he'd said.

"I know men who are not nearly as wealthy as you. In material terms, they don't have what you have. But they are more fulfilled than you are, many times over, because they don't have tangible assets."

"You're not understanding me. I just don't give a hoot about recognition or titles—let alone what anyone or any 'authority' thinks of me."

Bernard thought about what he was hearing. He quickly put it down to some lingering remnants of his son's adolescent days.

"Later on, you'll understand, my boy."

"We'll see. I'm not holding my breath."

"So then—back to the good news!"

"I'm keen to know. Don't keep me in suspense for another minute." David could hear his father thinking, *It would have been nicer if he'd left out that sarcastic tone.*

"No, my boy, it's not that easy."

There was a moment's silence, and then another. This dragged on so long that David checked to make sure his phone was still connected.

"By the way, we're going to the Classic Car Fair in the South together this weekend. "

David really couldn't give a fig about cars. At an early age, he'd abandoned the collection of toy cars he'd been given. For years, he was expected to like cars. He found himself several times a week among other boys of the same age amid toy cars, garages, and miniature car washes. For a while, he'd really given it a go, making engine noises, causing collisions, and all the rest. It quickly became clear it was all for naught.

"I know you don't care about cars. But everything around it is worth your time, including the news on the event. And maybe, just maybe, you'll decide to develop a love for these wonderful machines after all. I know you have a passion for machines."

David had to give him that. He did have a thing for all kinds of devices of all sizes: gears, semiconductors, robotics. But the way he saw it, that's not what cars were about at all. He'd been to car fairs before. The men around him blathered on about the horsepower, sometimes even throwing newton meters into the mix. But, in fact, they cared first and foremost about appearances and the logo on the steering wheel and the hubcaps. The entire topic might have stood a better chance if people had talked to him about cylinders, coolers, and fuel efficiencies. But he realized pretty quickly that neither colors nor shapes held any interest for him, let alone the brand name.

"I'm sorry—I'm just not a car fair person." This was a level of honesty that David hardly ever showed his father.

"I'm telling you again, the news alone makes it worth it."

David took his time before answering. Was this the moment to stand firm, to take charge of what he would and wouldn't say yes to? He found it hard to disappoint his father. On the other hand, wasn't that what his father done to him for the most part? How many birthdays had he physically been to—not just by making a phone call, sending him a card, or buying him a big, flashy gift that was more about how much it was worth and how outsized it was than about how much the young David would like it? In his rooms, he'd had countless toy cars and army toys that were still waiting to be assembled or glued together. Some of them still lay unopened. Others he had sold online as soon as people stopped asking him about them. The transaction was ultimately the only pleasure he had derived from many of them.

"I obviously want to hear the news, but I'm sorry. I just have no interest at all in cars, and I'll never be able to change that."

Bernard sighed without putting his hand over the phone. David heard it loud and clear.

"Maybe we can do something else—just have a bite to eat. I have time now. It's on me. Let me just check my diary." Bernard noisily flicked through the thick pages of his diary. "I can move some things around. I always make time for you. I know a very nice bistro that's located between us. I haven't been there in years. Shall I make a reservation?"

"Sure. Just send me the address, and I'll be there in an hour."

David walked to his wardrobe. Everything in him didn't want to conform. He would have preferred to wear his gray jogging pants and keep on his black T-shirt rather than putting on a dress shirt. Yet it was as if his arms and legs had acted on their own and decided for him. He watched as his limbs dutifully picked out a pair of neatly pressed pants and a shirt, as well as a matching pair of leather shoes, from his closet.

He felt his phone vibrate. The bistro had a difficult-to-pronounce French name. Luckily, he could pronounce the street name. He clicked on the address and ordered a taxi, timing things so that he would arrive just in time.

*       *       *

Within half an hour, the metamorphosis was complete. He had gone from a scruffy coder-type to debonair catch. It was like going on a blind date, even though it was anything but. He even smelled good—something his father wouldn't even appreciate. He was going to a French restaurant with his father to receive news that could only disappoint. He had resolved not to think about what it could be. Any kind of effort would have a low return on investment; it could only be disappointing.

His phone vibrated again. The taxi, he was told, would be there in two minutes or less. David knew that it would take longer than that to get to the pick-up point, even though it was all within the gates of his home. He typed a message to the driver that he was on his way, even as he jogged toward him.

"Good morning."

"Nice place. Do you work here?"

"Yes, for a rich family."

"Do you do their books for them?

"Yeah, something like that."

David and the driver didn't exchange another word. Enough had been said.

*     *     *

"What did I tell you?" Bernard asked when David arrived at the restaurant.

"Yes, it's a nice place." As far as David was concerned, there was hardly anything about the bistro to distinguish it from so many of the restaurants he'd been to. He'd had a big kitchen built in his house, and he had the money to have a really good chef working for him there. He lived on home deliveries, though—mainly pizza, sometimes Chinese food, and once or twice a week a poke bowl to try to compensate for the other unhealthy food.

"Just the Malbec and a jug of water from the tap please. Both of us will take the set menu, and please take some extra time after the third dish."

David found it a bit strange that he liked how his father had taken it upon himself to place the order. The risk of getting something that was less tasty than the other choices was small, and he was glad he hadn't spent time reading the menu in advance. That's why he had built a feature into the RoboWok machines early on that chose a dish completely at random. After some time, the choice was based on the customer's previous ordering behavior and on the prices of the ingredients that day. He'd been saying for months that he expected most customers to use this feature within a few years. To his amazement, though, people continued to make all the choices, even though, according to the data, it turned out to be the same choice for many loyal customers, again and again.

"Not far from your home, right?"

"No, just a short ride."

A long, drawn-out silence followed. David spent the time putting various spreads on the rolls in the basket of bread they'd been given when they came in. He took his time putting way too much butter on the last ones. After he had done each piece, he scraped the crumbs off the edge of the table into one hand and tipped them into the ashtray in the center. Smoking had been banned for years in this kind of place, so it was odd that there was an ashtray there at all, he thought.

An amuse-bouche followed. The waiter told them in detail what was on the spoon. It seemed to David to be too much work to put into such a small morsel. His father, however, listened attentively and nodded approvingly.

They both took a bite. Then, for almost a minute, his father went on about how much he had liked the morsel.

"So is this news going to be revealed soon?"

"News?"

"The news you were going to tell me."

"Oh, yes. That news. Well of course. Have a bit more of this delicious soup, and then I'll tell you. Take your time to really enjoy the soup. Don't speculate too much about what the news might be."

"I'll do my darnedest." It was a white lie, which he told just to be telling it. David had no intention of spending any time guessing what the news might be.

The soup seemed to take an age to come. They had eaten all the bread, and David had carefully tipped all the crumbs neatly into the ashtray and rearranged the salt and pepper shakers several times, giving each of them the best spot on the table. He found the long silence really discomfiting and thought it was equally strange that Bernard seemed to have no problem with it at all.

"Ah yes, the soup. This is what people come here for."

David found it hard to imagine that people would come to any restaurant just for the soup.

Maybe for the other courses—a very nicely prepared cut of meat, a deliciously brewed coffee, or a cake that was a famous pastry chef's *pièce de résistance*—but a soup? A soup can score a seven out of ten at the most. David had had many soups, and there wasn't a single one he could remember.

"Very tasty indeed."

It was an onion soup. It tasted like onion soup. It tasted like all of the other onion soups he had ever had. The best part was the bread and grilled cheese that were floating in it.

They finally finished their soups.

"I won't keep you in suspense any longer."

"Good! I'm keen to hear the news." David had actually been planning on going to the toilet, but he decided not to take the risk of having to wait longer for the news.

"I'm very excited to be able to share this. I myself had to wait more than two decades for it. But because I've used my network, you won't have to wait anything like that long. Really, my boy, this is fantastic news."

"Don't leave me in suspense for another single minute." Again, the sarcasm had proven difficult to hide.

"Oh now, steady on. You have to realize what this is. How much it will be worth to you. I remember well when it was my moment. It was just magnificent and quite compelling. I can't imagine life without it."

David had to admit to himself that he was getting a little curious. It almost sounded like it might be some kind of operation—a stomach reduction or some technology your eye could be fitted with that would make your vision twice as good.

"So, then, I won't keep you in suspense any longer. You can also take a bit of credit for it yourself, even though that bit was also arranged personally by me. But after your lecture, the committee has decided to accept your application."

"Application?" He had no idea what his father was going on about.

"Yes, my boy. Your father has seen to it that you can join. As perhaps the youngest member ever."

Now the penny dropped. "Fantastic news. Really fantastic."

"Fantastic isn't the word, my boy. You're going to love it."

"Do I have to do anything for it?"

"Most of it is done for you. There's an induction twice a year. You've been added for the next one, at the end of the summer. All you've got to do is show up."

"Fantastic news." David thought that he was very good at hiding his true feelings.

"And better yet, the first year is on the house. They're trying to attract younger members. Old men like me are queuing up."

"Fantastic news."

# 13. NATASHA

Not long ago, she was proud of not needing an alarm clock. She had all sorts of old college friends who shared the most impressive feats on social media. This marathon, that triathlon. Traveling around the world, even building a house. Natasha hadn't done anything like that, and in most cases, she had neither the wish nor the ability to do so. Her work was her calling, and, unlike all those sporty types, that meant that she didn't need an alarm clock in the morning. Until now, at least.

Recently, she'd gotten one. An old-fashioned digital clock, with red stripes on a dark brown—once black—background that together formed four numbers. She had first set the old device to a radio station with the news—it seemed like a good idea to wake up to the latest news. However, the pleasantly deep voice of the DJ who read the news had proved ineffectual at waking Natasha, which was the whole point of the exercise, so she switched to the loudest, most irritating squeak she could find. She got complaints about it from many housemates who would go to bed much later and who had to get up much later. Initially, the beep had worked. It had done enough to wake her up, until she found a way, in auto-pilot mode, to slap the snooze button.

This particular morning, she lost count of the number of times she did that and was unable, mentally or physically, to look at the clock. If she'd had to guess, she would have said she'd pressed the button seven or eight times already, if not more. Each press of the button bought her nine more minutes. Her sense of urgency was set firmly to OFF. Her body had determined that the reason for getting out of bed no longer outweighed the happiness of lying in, in extra intervals of nine minutes. She felt how effort- lessly her hand slapped the snooze button on her behalf, right on target every time, without her having to as much as open one eye. Another down payment of nine minutes.

She would never have gotten out of bed with just the help of the alarm clock. It was the constant vibrating of her phone somewhere that got her out of bed.

She managed this with considerable difficulty. The floor of her once tidy room was strewn with clothes and magazines. Her magazines were also back in her life. They had been out of her life since she was about sixteen, but they had now made a comeback.

She stumbled toward the vibration. She found her phone under an old hoodie and a rather large pile of socks.

There were thirty-nine unread messages.

She had not been used to this for a long time. She had once been knee-deep in operations. There was a separate app installed on her phone that let her know if a machine somewhere was not working as planned, if a delivery had not been made on time or, worse yet, if an important ingredient was out of stock. At the time, she would not have been shocked by a paltry thirty-nine new messages. Better still, she had gotten a load of positive adrenaline from numbers over one hundred—that meant a meaningful day and a slew of opportunities to add value.

She opened the messages. They were all from one sender—all short sentences with no punctuation in sight.

> *Where are you?*
>
> *I waited here for you for ages.*
>
> *I see you didn't fill in the questionnaire either.*
>
> *I have to submit your work in an hour.*
>
> *Results needed now.*
>
> *This is not acceptable.*
>
> *In all my years, this has never happened before.*

That was the last message she deigned to look at. She had to laugh. For all she knew, her new boss had worked for about a week before becoming her boss at RoboWok, so for that reason alone, it was really unlikely that he'd ever experienced anything like this before.

Not so long ago, but before RoboWok, getting a barrage of messages like this would have stressed Natasha out to no end. She would have thrown on something and dashed off without a second thought. She was a classic "insecure overachiever," the emphasis being on "insecure." She'd decided at a young age that she was going to work harder than anyone else because she knew she'd never excel at anything based purely on her talent.

She had thought that this way of thinking would not last forever. However, she had also thought that she would gradually become mediocre and that she would care a little less about that each year.

However, it now appeared that she had gone from one hundred to zero in one fell swoop. The messages meant pretty much nothing to her. There she stood, still in her pajamas. No part of her felt any pressure to fly off to the office. That strange office, full of all those strangers. She knew every square meter, but it now felt like such an unfamiliar place.

She switched on the coffee machine. One of the good habits she had managed to hang onto was that, every night before she went to sleep, she would put a filter in the machine. She'd fill it with two tablespoons of coffee and the correlating amount of water. That way she would not have to press the switch in the morning. Usually, by the time she'd finished showering, a fresh cup of coffee would be waiting for her.

This morning, she took a much longer shower. As she stood there, she thought about the worst-case scenario. They could put her out on the street whenever they wanted. They could mete out the equivalent of some punishment. That wouldn't phase her at all. In a way, resigning might feel like a kind of liberation. All that had been done in the past few months was already the worst kind of punishment, in her opinion.

She dried herself off and put on her bathrobe. She took some skimmed milk from the fridge and her favorite mug from the cupboard. It was pink, with horses and rainbows on it. The guys at work thought it was cute that their only female colleague had a mug like this. She had taken the mug home as a keepsake just before RoboWok was taken over.

The day before, everything had felt heavy. Her body, her to-do list, her whole mind. She had not enjoyed the day at all. Not surprisingly, even the microwave dinner that night had also been very disappointing, and she had especially not been looking forward to the day after.

This was the great insight. It felt like a eureka moment. As if she had just discovered penicillin. She had nothing to look forward to. She created nothing, she worked toward nothing. Maybe for her bosses, but for her, there was nothing meaningful that she was working toward.

She had to solve this and solve it now. It just couldn't wait. All these to-do lists were meaningless. She would not throw them away, but before she would even consider looking at them, she had to, and would, define her objectives.

She thought for a moment of calling in sick and sending her password to her boss. That would give him access to all the answers he needed. But she decided not to. That would only be a stop-gap solution. She got dressed instead—an outfit that would be as out of place as possible if she did decide to go to work. From her desk drawer, she took out a stack of paper, and from her pencil case, which she had had for more than a decade, she took out a pen.

She left the house in an old T-shirt, even though it was at least jacket weather outside. She decided to go to the convenience store two streets away. Not a trendy café, but a place that mainly sold liquor in brown paper bags. She did not want to be distracted by people of her own generation with their hip possessions—by anything that would keep her attached to her salary.

She bought a can of mango juice, something she had never bought or drunk before, and sat down in the window. The owner had created a coffee corner in order to capture some market share in the world of high-margin coffee. The coffee, however, looked pretty awful, and mango juice was the first alternative she had seen out of the corner of her eye.

She picked up the sheets of paper she had brought with her, as well as her pen. What was she going to write down? What do you do in a case like this? Is writing the best thing to do, or would she not be better off walking or reading a book? She looked at the mango juice, the pile, and the paper.

No, she had to solve this now. She could not start thinking about optimal methodologies.

Her primary response was paper, pen, and her first can of mango juice. "This is what you have to do," she told herself. It was not as if she had never thought about goals before. She had even read a book about setting life goals, but neither the thinking nor the book had led to anything. Or rather, they had both led to this aimless existence.

She decided to draw two lines—something she remembered vaguely from a lecture she'd seen online. The two lines were axes. On the horizontal axis, she put "don't like" all the way on the left and "like" all the way on the right. She put "I'm good at" at the top of the vertical axis and "I'm not good at" at the bottom. In each quadrant, she started writing words—things she liked but that she was not good at. Things she did not like but that she was good at, and so on.

She noticed that her hand started writing almost automatically. Slowly, she saw how each quadrant was getting populated. The mango juice tasted good, her phone had stopped vibrating, and the piece of paper seemed to be filling up all on its own.

In no time at all, all the quadrants had been filled in quite nicely. The "not good at/don't like" quadrant was particularly well populated. All the words in it were related to the work she had been doing in the last few weeks—items such as "looking back," "fleshing out," and "putting together presentations."

The other three quadrants were much more interesting. It was clear she had to focus on things she liked and that she was best at.

She leaned back and looked outside for a moment. She repeated to herself, "Things I am good at that I like."

It seemed so simple. If she did things she liked and things she was good at, everything would work out. Everything she wanted to achieve would come naturally. If she did things she liked, it would take no effort at all, and she would not need an alarm clock. And if she was good at them, success would come naturally.

Soon, it was as if she was hearing her father's voice. "There's no such thing as a ten in life." Her father was not a pessimist—he was certainly a realist. Could she expect a life with all the fun things she was good at? She wanted life to be like that, but she also had to be realistic.

Perhaps the other two quadrants were more interesting. The things she was good at but that she did not like were the things she was being paid for. There's no ten, and you have to live on something. It was realistic, and she had to accept part of it in her life. So perhaps the fourth quadrant was the most interesting: things that she liked but that she was not good at.

Years earlier, she'd had a conversation with a girl not much older than she was who had spoken like a wise old guru. She had spoken of short- and long-term happiness. You would need both in life, she said, but they did not go hand in hand. Sometimes, she said, you have to sacrifice short-term happiness to achieve the long-term kind, and vice versa. This was so true, but she had not understood then how to apply this bit of wisdom, and she still didn't know now.

Everything seemed to be falling into place and coming together. It was a classic connect-the-dots moment, as Steve Jobs would have said. Her fourth quadrant was what she was focused on now—that and her sweet spot: things she was already good at and that she liked. The fourth quadrant was about things she liked but was not yet good at. Learning these skills would not bring her much happiness in the short term, but it would lead to what she now missed most—the feeling that she was doing something that would lead to long-term happiness.

All of these insights were giving her a huge amount of energy. Her body screamed for movement, and her mind was racing. It was as if the amount of information being processed was so great that her brain might implode at any moment.

She paid the owner of the convenience store, who looked as though he was always open and as though he employed only himself, and left the shop quickly. Under her arm was the completed piece of paper, and in the left corner of her mouth was the pen she'd used.

Once at home, she quickly did the laundry, including her bedding, which she hadn't washed for weeks. She opened her curtains for the first time in ages and filled the fridge with all kinds of fresh vegetables. She felt boundlessly energetic. The many insights she'd had and the feeling that her worst case was not so bad led her to the two quadrants in her matrix that indicated what she was good at and what she liked to do.

For the first time in a few hours, she sat down. She mashed half an avocado with an almost clean fork on a freshly toasted slice of wholemeal bread.

She picked up the sheet of paper and looked at her quadrants again. She zoomed in on her other important quadrant, which she'd named "investments"—things she liked but was not yet good at, the emphasis being on the *not yet*. She noticed that, of the four quadrants, this one was the least full. There were only a few words in it, ranging from the vague "self-discovery" to the very specific "coding."

She felt all of her energy quickly drain from her body. Yes, she had come up with a nice framework. She was quite clear about what she did not like and could not do well. But her most important quadrant had almost nothing in it— nothing that pointed specifically to a solution.

She took a bite of her sandwich, made another one-woman cup of coffee, and stared out the window. The world had woken up, and people were rushing toward their aimlessness.

Was the framework the right one? Did it solve the big questions? And which questions *were* these?

Was the idea mainly to find out what kind of work she should do—an exercise of sorts to find the most suitable job description? Or was it about much more—about what direction her life should take and what she should do with her time, and not just professionally?

"Self-discovery" jumped out at her again. It could mean anything. Why had she written that? Wasn't discovery in and of itself the key? Or was it that she had been docile for the most part? It was true that up until now she had mainly done what she was told. Did she have an internal desire to determine the broad outlines herself? Or was it that she just wanted to do new things and discover places or things she didn't know yet? She was only too aware that, like many people of her generation, she had a really short attention span.

Maybe she wanted too much too soon. But could she expect to go from optimal framework to optimal solution in just a few short hours? Would she find her calling so soon—and not only that, but a career choice, right then and there? She knew that some people spent their whole lives trying to find the answers to questions of these kinds. Who was she to think she was going to pull that off in a single morning?

Maybe she should adjust her goals. On the basis of what she could do now, she would take a new path—use today's insights to choose a new direction. At least she knew it wasn't going to be what she was doing now. She wasn't going to last years in this life—maybe not even weeks.

What could she do next month? How could she move faster along this path and arrive more quickly at insights that would lead her to her short- or long-term happiness? She could get a new job or start a business. Soon she was thinking in particular about the disadvantages of these options. They would both be long-term choices. She couldn't just keep changing jobs every month. The next choice she made would be for a few years at least, especially if she chose the entrepreneurial path.

Maybe she should do something shorter-term first—perhaps doing an assignment some-where or taking a trip.

She never admitted it, but secretly she had always looked down on people who traveled around the world. She had always found backpacking to be ostrich-like behavior. People who wanted to have nothing to do with real life and who put off doing anything meaningful.

She found the whole idea really clichéd, especially for someone like her. She would be the umpteenth person in her generation to travel at the first setback instead of going for actual solutions.

*On the other hand,* she thought to herself, *clichés don't become clichés just like that.* Like a lot of other people, she'd always been bothered by clichés. Her sense was that they were for people who didn't want to take the time to really have an opinion or experience something themselves. They sucked all the life out of meetings and never led to decisions of any real value. But she now realized that some clichés had become clichés for a reason. They had started as someone's opinion or insight. But as more and more empirical evidence of the predictive value of thought had come to light, they had become clichés.

The morning had led to great insights, a framework she was proud of. But perhaps the greatest victory was realizing that she had to embrace clichés. Perhaps she should use what humankind had already learned. She would not make any long-term decisions—it was simply too early. She would focus on a short-term solution, something where she could learn something about herself without being stuck for years. She would give her quadrants more focus by living, by having experiences—by taking a journey or finding a new environment. What did it matter that she too would be living this cliché? Not everything had to be on social media.

# 14. MARIA

She had spent many nights online. To the left of the mouse that controlled the arrow on the screen was a list of cryptic descriptions of her boss's treasures.

"Space lens" referred to an expensive-looking device she had found. That was all she knew about it. She had written down the make and model number—not "space lens." A master criminal would never do that.

It turned out to be virtual-reality glasses. When she read about the possible ways of using them, she had dreamed for a moment. With such a device, she could be close to both of her worlds. At home, but virtually, and at her place of work with everything but her mind and her eyes. It gave her hope for the future, but she could not dream for too long. *Dreamers*, she thought, *are not doers*. And she would have to be a doer to achieve her greater goal. A lifetime of dreaming would lead nowhere.

She found out online that the "space lens" in question was quite unique. It was part of a product line that had recently been discontinued. Because the company hadn't survived, the production run had been limited, and this model in particular had soon gathered something of a cult following.

There were special websites that collectors had created and videos in which monologues were made about the possibility of owning the device. Apparently, the company had ceased to exist because the device had become obsolete on every front and had been beaten on price to boot. *Funny,* she thought, *how there can be a demand for something that's inferior just because it's scarce.*

She'd picked up and held quite a few of these items. Some were simply too big or too heavy. Some seemed to have been used too recently. Maria figured that this would increase the chances that her boss would look for them.

In the end, she had not only put the virtual-reality device on her list but had also written down the specs on two watches and then moved them, along with a few figurines, some more miniature electronics items, and something that looked like the beginnings of a coin collection.

She'd written everything down cryptically and then moved each item to a place where she could check whether anyone would notice it without the item's leaving the house, as well as a spot in which, in step two, she could easily reach the object from outside and then take it home.

She had been fighting with herself lately. Approving theft by calling oneself a master criminal did not feel right. Everyone she looked up to was living, or had lived, an honest life. No theft, no disloyalty, no misuse of funds.

She had started making lists in her mind—of her heroes and, especially, her heroines. All of them were good people—no major transgressions. Yet she'd also noticed that they had not had the same responsibilities. They often had an existence that allowed them to live with their poverty. She, too, could easily have accepted that. She could live perfectly well without luxury. Unfortunately, though, she had several people depending on her. Besides, her heroines could live full-time for a purpose. She quickly realized that there was no comparison between her situation and theirs. All she could do was clean. There was no other full-time option available. Purpose and dependency: do they make it OK to steal stuff?

Maria didn't have an answer to that, and she decided to put off trying to find one. Perhaps she could make up for her misdeeds by giving back in other ways, like a modern-day Robin Hood. She also told herself that she could regard the proceeds of what she would steal as the salary she should rightly have earned. What is it, she asked herself, that makes cleaning a house less valuable than opening bank accounts? Were her hours worth less than those put in by someone who had learned to apply the law? Maria found several justifications for her plans in the making. She knew that the world would not agree, but the world would never have to know because her method was foolproof.

And it was this that frightened Maria the most. She felt a genuine sense of pride at the way she had handled the project. Yes, maybe it was theft, but she had elevated it to a serious craft.

And she had a further insight: She had often seen films in which future bosses of criminal organizations had started out small. And then things got out of control. When things were small-scale, the future boss was happy and didn't hurt society too much. Only when the future bosses, who were often men, became too avaricious and started building organizations did things start to go belly up. The trick for her was to know when to stop. And it couldn't be at the expense of anyone's happiness. As long as she was able to make a big leap in terms of her happiness while someone else was hardly affected, things would be better overall. It was justifiable, even though she knew that the ortho-dox view was that theft can never be justified.

That evening, she looked through her list again. She checked everything: Had she taken what was most valuable? Had it been moved long enough without being noticed? She had worked out from the cleaning calendar exactly who would be working when and where. There was a day when no one would be working in the room where her treasures lay while she was working outside near the treasure room. *Perfect,* she thought. She'd expected to have options and that she would have to weigh up which days to choose, but this day turned out to be simply more appropriate than any other.

She went to bed feeling good, justifying to herself for the umpteenth time what she was about to do. She had checked all the steps and knew exactly what to do and when. It was a fool-proof plan and more or less risk-free. Neverthe-less, she had difficulty falling asleep that night. The plan was perfect, and the victim would not suffer one bit. What kept her awake were thoughts of her home. What would they think of her? Or if she grew old and had the chance to look back on her life, what would she think of herself? She would be proud because, despite her humble beginnings, she would have lived a financially stable life, regardless of how she'd gotten there. Or would she make herself and the people she cared about infinitely prouder if she had been a good person and had learned to cope with all the setbacks?

The subject became heavier and heavier in her mind. She knew that she desperately needed the hours of sleep and that such off-work hours were precious. Her body was screaming "tired," but her mind found it more important to think. What was the purpose of these decades on earth? Was it maximizing the happiness of the individual, or of the world, or of one's offspring? Was happiness now worth more than looking back with pride, from your deathbed, at a hard life?

She saw herself, an old woman, stooped over from all the honest hours spent cleaning and now on her deathbed, ready to leave this world but still with a few days of clarity to look back and reflect on what she could have done better and what she'd done well. Would she ever have the chance to put herself under the microscope like that? What an investment, a whole life of being honest and good, only to find that, during this evaluation, it was all for naught. Or perhaps there wouldn't even *be* this moment of evaluation. Was she living, then, just for the afterlife? If so, she needed to know what the point was of living without any days of happiness after her youth had been spent. Had she been put on earth to clean someone's house cost-effectively? Was she a kind of angel to her family so that she could have her "great deeds" serve as a legacy? She preferred to think of life as a gift that you had to use to the best of your abilities. Only then would the gift giver be happy at having chosen you as the recipient.

Accumulated happiness—that was it. Certainly with deep valleys that served as an investment for peaks of happiness both big and small—that's what it was all about. The sum of these peaks minus the negative days still had to be in positive territory, with a preference for a peak today or tomorrow. What if it were in five or ten years' time? Would she still be there then? In what capacity?

Everything in her head kept automatically justifying her choices. The thought that kept her awake more than any other was simple, though difficult to resolve—the chance that this would all go horribly wrong and that she would be caught *in flagrante delicto*. It didn't matter how small the chance was, or how perfect her plan, or how limited the impact on her boss would be. The consequences could be out of proportion to any of that. And then, of course, she might have a criminal record. This was the worst-case scenario. In her case, it would destroy any chance of employment. And worse yet, the big question was whether she would be allowed to stay. All those years of suffering had at least given her family something priceless. She could make her own life more bearable by doing what she was planning, but she could still ruin the lives of her loved ones or at least bring them to the point she had started out from—but without the options she had had.

Profit could mean more happiness, except perhaps when it came to looking back on everything from her deathbed. Still, she made her peace with that. If things went badly, that would reduce her chances here from almost nothing to less than nothing, but she would not be the only one affected.

She thought of what it would be like to go back home with nothing to show for all her efforts but a criminal record. As much as she could justify it to herself, she would be pegged as a criminal. She'd walk around with a label for the rest of her life, and so would those closest to her.

# 15. NATASHA

If the last weeks of her life were to be filmed, Natasha thought, it would be the most disappointing sequence of scenes in movie history.

Was there ever a movie where the main character had a eureka moment but then just went back to work? The same alarm clock, the same breakfast, the same service rendered to a group of people who were miles from everything she stood for, or at least wanted to stand for.

It would be pure dreck. Perhaps she was an almost invisible extra in some really gripping film. RoboWok deserved more than one movie—a trilogy, perhaps. But she might have a few quick frames in minute eighty-two of part two, somewhere in a corner, obviously without speaking. Her part would be played by an actress who was finally allowed to be an extra after ten years of auditions, only to become a waitress.

Her heart, her brain, almost everything had seemed to say goodbye to this life. However, it was as if her legs and, to a degree, her hands disagreed and had been abusing their power over Natasha's body for weeks. The alarm clock had gone off, and her limbs had proceeded in workaday fashion to get her into her work clothes and then to walk her, like a Thunderbirds marionette, to the place she had developed such a loathing for.

And it was not just her limbs—her mouth had now also gotten in on the act. Once back, she'd actually apologized to her superiors and her colleagues and more or less begged for another chance, even putting on a show of being grateful when clemency had been granted.

She had been so close; she had mapped out the entire route. She had started making lists of buildings and natural phenomena she wanted to see and had drawn up a list of activities. She had plotted all of this out on a globe with a lamp inside, which she had bought for less than a cup of coffee at a shop that sold globes directly from pallets, as well as washing racks, buckets, and a huge variety of cleaning cloths.

She'd put all the round, red stickers on the globe. Then she'd indicated with different colors where the best season was in terms of climate, crowds, and prices. It had become a complex multidimensional matrix of stickers on a sphere. If it were ever unearthed thousands of years after her death, scientists would study it for years to find patterns and dissect new mathematical magic.

Natasha had gone so far as to find out not only when and where but also how and what to eat. Breakfast, teatime, lunch, drinks, and dinner. She would have been proud of her globe and the spreadsheets that went with it were it not for the fact that the detail was all about a very particular way of fleeing.

Even after the when-and-where phase, she'd started looking for tickets. Version one of her plan had involved a number at least four times higher than what she had thought. She had played all kinds of extremely complex tricks to get the price down to three times what she was willing to pay. She'd made complex routes in which she chose destination X via stopover Y but would get off at Y. She'd selected buses between airports in faraway countries and used air miles she'd already earned on one leg of the trip for a later leg. She'd installed a VPN so she could make it seem from her laptop that she was in India or China, and thus avoid European prices. These were all small breakthroughs, but the end result was disappointing.

She had the money for the tickets, and she would have money for hostels, food, and activities. She had worked it out. She had even found places where she could work, for a small fee or in return for bed and breakfast. She had already overcome the biggest barrier without any effort. The budget was just there.

At several points she let her finger hover over the "Buy now" button, her mouse under one hand, her credit card in the other. The first time, she had thought of applying for another credit card at the last minute. Partly, or in fact mostly, for the sake of postponing everything. But also so as to have another way to save points, to get the costs down even lower. It had taken her a week to find the right credit card deal, one that offered a lot of points and no fees for the first year. And then she had dutifully waited for the plastic card to arrive through her door. Not that she needed the card physically—the credit card company had already given her all the details to start buying things.

She had then started putting the trip together again, with a strange kind of hope that the tickets would be more expensive now so she would have an excuse to put off clicking "Buy now." But unfortunately—it had really felt like a shame—it had become even cheaper, especially when she bought all the tickets from what her VPN made the internet believe was India.

She did not understand herself. The trip was perfect. Each destination had been carefully chosen and well timed. She had read up on hundreds of destinations and activities and selected only those that she felt really excited to read about. The timing was miraculously achievable: of all her destinations, she was able to see more than 90 percent at exactly the right moment. Perfect weather, with not too many people, and all quite affordable.

She just did not understand herself. She wanted this, she could do it, and it fit into her new life strategy. How hard could it be? The stumbling block was the fear of coming back. What would she be able to do once she returned? What options would she have left? Employers would see that she'd taken all this time off, and she would immediately stand out from all the other candidates who had not embarked on a world tour so early, who were ambitious and who showed that they had what it takes.

RoboWok had been everything to her, her higher calling. But what would the market think of it? "Just another start-up sold to a corporate company." They would probably think that she had just been futzing around. She had come on board precisely because it was a start-up. They had had a hard time finding people within their budget, so they hired Natasha for next to nothing.

What were the chances of her finding such a company again when she got back? Pretty slim—she would have to compete with better options in a much tighter labor market. She saw it all for herself: all kinds of travel stories to tell, but after rejections five and six, it would be back to square one with little money and even fewer prospects.

She would have to take side jobs, burn her hands on hot plates, and put up with nagging customers. "Where is my ketchup?" "Does this have gluten in it?" "We're still waiting on those extra fries." "Sorry, this orange juice doesn't *taste* fresh."

She would be that woman who had once lived a little—who'd seen the world, only to spend the rest of her life barely making ends meet.

There were also evenings when she was more hopeful. Perhaps she would fall in love in a distant land. Or perhaps she would not find the job of her dreams, but in the worst-case scenario, she would at least be able to reorganize her life. She was on her own and healthy. She could go and live in a country where she could even buy a piece of land, with a tiny house on it, with the money she had left. She could rent it out, get to know the neighborhood, and give tours. That would be just enough to live on. Because what did she really need after all?

A bed, a bucket, a gas stove, and a place where she could stay warm and dry. She had often played the worst-case scenario back in her mind. On her piece of land with almost no other possessions. It actually began to appeal to her more and more. The simplicity—exactly what she needed. A little bit of stress about money, but she'd have just enough for her basic needs. She could tuck into a nice cut of meat, with her own home-grown vegetables on the side.

So what was stopping her? She could travel, come back, and try to live the worst-case scenario, which was now beginning to seem far from worst case. It was even starting to become best case—and certainly preferable to city life with a city job.

Today it was as if karma was trying to help her. It was one of those days when everything seemed to go wrong from the start. It had been raining, and the window had not been properly closed. The bottom of her blanket and the top of her curtains were soaking wet.

She'd had to wait for two others at the shower, only to take a shower that could hardly even be called lukewarm.

Then she'd rushed off to work. The wait for the shower had meant she'd had to jump into her clothes without having eaten and then run for her bus.

Once at work, she rushed straight to the coffee machine. This was to be the moment when everything would turn around for her, when the bad would become good. Coffee would be a natural border between bad luck and happiness.

She grabbed the coffee from the machine and walked toward her seat. Around her seat, her colleagues, some of whom she still didn't know, were busy with something that recalled nothing in her brain.

She sat down and blew into her coffee, as if that might instantly bring it to the desired temperature.

"Good morning."

Natasha was startled and automatically sat up straight, feeling for all the world like a well-trained schoolgirl at a Catholic girls' boarding school.

"Um, good morning."

"You are lucky."

For a moment, Natasha thought something nice was about to happen. Her supervisor did not know sarcasm or any other low forms of wit. Lucky had to mean straight-up good fortune. Coffee had indeed been a natural border between bad luck and happiness.

"I had forgotten about it for a while, but the work you delivered to us from our first weeks together . . ."

*Our first weeks together*, thought Natasha. It sounded as if they had started a life together. This was a way of thinking that made her really uncomfortable. It was his life that she was serving—there was no "togetherness" about it. Even if she had the option of bringing "togetherness" into it, she did not want to think about that.

"Sorry, can you say that again?"

"Management wants you to do over the work you've done."

"What work?"

Her manager plopped the plasticized document on her desk. The document with way too many pages, in which she had described too many processes. The hardest thing she had ever done, not because of its complexity but because of her reluctance. Every page had been a trauma.

"Management wants to map out new processes?" Natasha suddenly felt a strange mix of fear, surprise, and misery.

"We are not much further along, but as you know, everything has been turned around. Everything is different."

"There have indeed been many changes." Natasha actually had no idea what her supervisor was talking about. The people seemed to be the same—they were all in the same place and all seemed to be doing similar things.

"How much time do you need? You have the expertise under your belt now. It should be faster than last time."

"Of course." Natasha's mouth had acted on its own again. Every other part of her had shouted, "No!"

The work itself was beyond tedious, truly awful—a hellish job that would take weeks and without any payoff at the end. There would be no satisfaction to be had from it. She knew that from the first time around. But worst of all, she knew that, this time around too, no one would read it. There was even a chance that only her manager would hold the document and that no other person would see it, let alone crack it open. Even her manager had only looked at the cover.

What malevolent forces were behind all of this? Who would want to get this done, knowing full well that nobody was actually waiting to get their hands on it? They simply wanted to keep her busy. Was she the legacy of the acquisition who needed to be kept occupied? If they had signed a contract to keep Natasha on and occupied, even with busy work, it would have been a condition of purchase.

That was the worst. She could do so much more than this. She had shown that time and again, at the very same company. RoboWok may have had a new owner, but the service was exactly the same. They had launched a loyalty program to a lot of fanfare, but apart from that, all the changes were internal. Organization charts, processes, weekly routines, and paper—a lot of paper. The end customer saw the same machine and ate the same meals.

In her time at the company, she had contributed to those meals. They had listened to customers and adjusted the amount of meat and made the sauce thinner. She had led a project to offer more payment options. These were all things that had created value, for both customers and RoboWok.

That had disappeared. And worse yet, of all the bullshit jobs, she'd gotten the bullshittiest. It was a bit of useless, time-consuming work that no one would see or care about.

# 16. DAVID

David had paced endlessly around his house, down long corridors, around the gym, through the kitchens, tracing new routes for the sake of variety that was starting to wear thin.

One morning he'd made fresh coffee three times, only to drink just the one tiny espresso. He had also thrown the occasional basketball through a hoop, although the proportion of baskets to attempts had proven to be even lower than that of coffees made to coffees drank.

The emptiness was driving him around the bend. He would wake up, then lie in bed for an hour, staring at the ceiling. Then he'd usually take another hour to have his shower, until he got hungry. He'd have breakfast made—a full breakfast to fill up the day. The rest of the morning, which often spilled over into afternoon, consisted of chowing down, wandering around, sometimes watching a film or unpacking a recent purchase, invariably an item that added not a whit of value to his life.

This morning was different. He'd woken up much earlier, and his body had sent him to the shower almost immediately. He'd taken a much shorter shower than usual—hardly a major achievement in itself, to be sure.

The insight was so simple and so obvious. It was bizarre that this had not happened before. It had been a long time since a thought—just a thought—had made him snap awake and become so alert. It was as if a higher power had breathed new energy into him.

The idea: do it all again. RoboWok was epic. It had transformed such a large industry, been such a business success, and also helped make people healthier. All of that had been shown by an independent third party. The food was so well priced that a whole section of the population that would normally go to their nearest burger joint had started eating meals with vegetables.

He had unconsciously clung to the idea that something so significant was no longer possible, that there were no industries left in which such a disruption was possible—that it had all been done or was being done, or that the barriers to entry were so high that even with his newfound wealth, he wouldn't stand a chance.

But this new understanding was much different. Industries could also be transformed on a different scale and have smaller, or different, kinds of collateral impact. He had been put on the earth to provide solutions that would meet consumer needs better than any agency or person had managed so far, regardless of the industry or the scale of the solution.

This had opened up so many possibilities. He had been systematically going through one industry after another and striking them off as he went: aviation, hospitality, entertainment. None of them gave him any bright ideas. So now he'd switched to a more straightforward question—what do people want? Or better yet—what do *most* people want?

He had once started with the most basic form of a customer's wish: food. He had gone back to thinking about food. Why do people eat? How do they eat? How do they get their food? Thinking back from the mouth all the way to the beast or the piece of land made it clear to him that there was so much inefficiency in the supply chain. He was going to be a food expert.

Yeah, right. Still, it was clear that, if he used his smarts, a lot could be improved, and a lot could be gained.

He did not write—he just repeated activities in his head: eating, living, doing sports, sleeping, caregiving. Each time a new activity popped into his head, he hoped that it would be the seed that could lead to an understanding of how to fulfill some customer need better than anyone else was doing now. He was really hoping to take an industry that was steeped in dogmas and grab it by the scruff of the neck.

That was actually his *raison d'être*: to overthrow dogmas. Religion was easy; he'd been able to defuse that dogma in his teens. When it came to industry, though, things were quite different.

When he had first started talking to so-called food experts, he was met with laughter, or sometimes a blank stare. What did he know about the industry? Men in their fifties, mostly white, waffled on and on about their experience in the food-and-beverage industry. They told him they'd seen it all before and wanted to save him from the mistakes they themselves had made.

He remembered a representative who was so full of himself and who called himself something with "senior" and "consultant" in it. When the "senior consultant" heard of a window behind which meals were prepared, he began telling a story about a company from twenty years before. It was a wall in which hot meals were placed every day. Customers could drop their coins in and pick up ready-to-eat hot meals. He said it had worked, but that it had been a small, unhealthy niche. Customer experience, he said, was everything. His intentions were good, but it was clear he hadn't heard a word of David's pitch, which included just that example. David had even made the particular point that this experience had been the starting point for him. People would see the meal being prepared from products that were always fresh. As with any dogma, the man had listened only to those "truths" he already knew. He simply couldn't hear any other perspectives or insights.

David started his list again: eat, live, exercise, sleep, dress.

Dress up, dress down.

This verb and its phrasal variant did something to him. He'd always found fashion and everything that went with it reprehensible. How could one pay more for the same fabric but with an Italian or French name embroidered on it? How could people base their entire lives around reviving old trends? Reviving! It was the opposite of everything he stood for. Progress, progress, and more progress—the rest was unimportant.

David phoned a person somewhere in the house. He had no idea who it was or where they were. He knew only that, at the other end of the line, there was someone whose job it was to bring him things.

He asked for a stack of A2 sheets and very simple black ballpoint pens. He reiterated that they had to be black, not blue and certainly not red.

He just couldn't wait, so he picked up an unread magazine from a step. The first page he tore out was mostly white. Funnily enough, it was a fashion ad.

His first sketch, if that's what it could be called, was of a value chain. Wikipedia came into play in it. Where do materials come from? How are they processed? Where do they go? What's done manually, and what's done by machines? What links are there—especially the needless ones? Where did the brands begin?

For a moment, he thought about a platform. Couldn't he connect all those brands and a platform to a place closer to the source? He could find the origins for materials in poor, low-wage countries, and then group them into a platform where brands only have to upload their design.

*That's too obvious,* he thought. It was too normal an idea—something any budding entrepreneur would come up with. He was worried not only about the competition but especially about his stress levels. He did not have to do it for the money. He had to be entertained, and while he was at it, change an industry for the consumer. And more important still—this was always a must—he had to think big, in terms of both turnover and goals. He had to become Robin Hood and Henry Ford rolled into one. And it had to be complex enough; it shouldn't be possible to draw it on an A4 sheet, or in his case, A2 sheets, in a single afternoon. It would take him just a week to have a platform built. The rest would be uninteresting sourcing and marketing work.

Just one more coffee—he needed a bigger sheet of paper after all. He took his time over this cup, to prepare it as well as actually consume it. He could have coffee made by the people downstairs, but preparing it himself made drinking it so much more enjoyable.

In the distance, he heard a rumble and a series of doors being opened. A few minutes later, a stack of A2 sheets and a box of black ballpoint pens were in front of him. Perfect.

The cup of coffee gave him an idea: he had to think the other way around. He started from a point he knew and that had brought him success before. At RoboWok, everything had started with the consumer and their experience. The back end had come only later. With predictable needs for ingredients and predictable volumes, he could do the procurement better and closer to the source. This was cheaper, better for farmers since there would be no inter-mediaries, and better for the world. But all of this had come much later.

Again, he had to put himself in the consumer's shoes. He drew a figure—barely a stick figure. Intuitively, he drew a circle around the figure. Where did people buy clothes?

He sketched online platforms, shops, catwalks. It was a world he didn't know well at all. Yet he felt comfortable with what he knew—it wasn't rocket science. You didn't have to be a restaurateur to understand restaurants—everyone knows Mickey D's. It was the same sort of thing. Everyone needed clothes at some point. And everyone had been to a store for a sweater or a pair of pants.

The drawing led nowhere. There was still a lot of room on the sheet of white A2 paper. David said sorry to the world and especially, out loud, to the trees, and picked up a new sheet.

He began with a question that was much closer to his heart: "What's aggravating about buying clothes?"

Going to the shop, having an opinion on fashion, finding the right size, standing in line at the checkout, realizing when you get home that you picked the wrong size, clothes going out of fashion, and trying on clothes.

He stopped. Trying on clothes. It was the closest thing to a eureka moment he'd had since RoboWok. He'd always hated trying on clothes. Especially fitting rooms and the moment when you had to ask for a smaller or bigger pair of jeans. Calling out through the fitting-room curtain. Once he had even bought trousers that were too big, only because he felt that that was better than having to try on yet another pair in that cramped little cubicle.

The internet had already made his life better. No more going to clothing shops. He bought clothes only when he had to. He bought the most cost-effective clothing options with as little printed matter on them as possible and almost always with no visible branding. When in doubt, he ordered several sizes with the idea of returning the surplus one day.

This had to be done better. Ordering more sizes, having to take time to look at clothes, trying on items at home—all of these steps were unnecessary.

Fortunately, he also quickly realized that there were people who did like fashion, hard as that was to imagine—people who needed to show off what brands they were wearing, who thought that having an Italian brand name on their chest would increase their personal worth, or at least help them project an air of greater confidence. There were also people who liked browsing clothes endlessly and could not wait to see what the latest fashion was.

But trying on clothes. David could not think of any group of people who liked trying things on. This was a perfect starting point— make it unnecessary to try things on. Once he had that down, the rest started to fall into place.

If he had the place where people bought clothes without having to try then on, then he would have the consumer. With him, you knew that everything would fit. Once he had volume, the rest would come: great selection, easier choices, better sourcing. The sky was the limit. (David resolved then and there never to use that expression again.)

In the days that followed, he read everything he could get his hands on about fashion, especially fashion technology. He printed out a number of articles and gave them a place on a new notice board he'd had his staff purchase. He read about where the costs and especially the revenues lay. He read about trend cycles and fashion seasons, about the large conglomerates behind many brands, which were precisely tailored to specific target groups but with the exact same operation on the back end.

One of the articles that stood out the most was on remnants. He knew about these from the food industry. At RoboWok, he spent a lot of time on regression analysis to minimize waste. A team calculated exactly how many meals would be sold based on historical data but also on external effects such as competitor prices and the weather. There were times when David opted to turn down consumers rather than throw away food.

In fashion, a huge number of yards are thrown away or shredded and burned every year by brands that do not want their branded clothing to end up on gray markets and that know when a season is over and when a collection will no longer contribute to their image.

On-demand clothing—that was what he was after. The technology was already there. It just needed to be scaled up. He spent half a day away from fashion, looking at 3D-printed houses and prosthetics. *Clothes, then, will surely be a piece of cake*, he thought. He would set up printer lines close to the customer and optimize them to cater to local demand and maximize the number of repeat customers. All inputs would be sustainable; he could get them directly from the source. He had only to distribute them to the print hubs, as he had already started calling them by now.

It was the first building block that was clear and more or less carved in stone. He would steer clear of any methods of operating that would put the stock at risk. This was the way forward—no question.

However, that in turn raised new questions. At the moment, clothes had to be tried on somewhere. He toyed with the idea of using algorithms to predict what people wanted to wear and sending it unsolicited. With the margins he would be able to make, it was no problem if people could indicate in an app that they did not want certain items. The consumer would even be allowed to keep it. Now *that* would be disruption!

He had enough sources for what was "in fashion." It was clear that, at least in the Western world, there were a limited number of themes.

One of the A2 sheets was used as a matrix for collecting themes. "Man," "woman," and "unisex" were on the vertical axis. All the themes he could think of for one or more of the three categories were on the horizontal axis. "Workwear," "Trendy," "Sporty flashy," "Sporty inconspicuous," "Gothic," "Bruce Springsteen-ish." He knew there must be better names for some of the themes he had in mind. But with the forty-six categories he managed to come up with, he could categorize most of the people in images he found at random online.

Yet he had the feeling that people wanted to make choices. People often do not realize that they fit into a certain box. They at least want to appear to be unique, even if they end up buying the same clothes from the same shop.

He toyed with the idea of opening shops that had just one exemplar of each item that people could select. They would then get a copy of it in a cubicle that was printed for their size and that would thus fit them perfectly.

He quickly dismissed the idea, however, as he wanted nothing to do with physical clothing shops and the chance of leftovers.

He was stuck. He had gone to watch a movie with a plot that was as empty as a plot could be and still bear the name. The movie was dominated by a bombastic soundtrack full of sound and fury and lots of gunfire. There was no room in his brain to follow a complex storyline. The stupider the better.

He could not stop his brain. During the movie, he thought, *What if I make every form of media shoppable? People watch films, read books, and see ads. What if they can print every item of clothing with the click of a button?*

It was not a bad idea, but he soon realized that it was more of a marketing tool. It was not the big idea that made the fitting unnecessary. People wanted to see themselves in the clothes.

People wanted to see *themselves* in the clothes. People wanted to see themselves, for themselves, in the clothes.

That was it! No eureka moment for years and now two in such quick succession. The whole idea of fitting was to see yourself in clothes. It was so simple. He simply had to have a method of sticking clothes on people, without physical clothes or physical people.

This was easy—augmented reality or virtual reality. It could even be done with old-fashioned photos of a person from multiple angles. The only problem he had to solve was scanning people. He had to have not only pictures of people but also exact measurements.

That night he slept in two blocks of two hours each. His brain did not stop. He had seen the entire fashion-related database of hyperlinks in Google by now. Now he was working on measurement technology. LiDAR, AR—all kinds of technologies crossed his mind. Each of them had its advantages and disadvantages. Each was feasible, but would it be precise and consistent enough? And what did he do with people who regularly changed sizes, such as children or yo-yo-dieting forty-somethings?

He had to find a solution. There was no deadline. The money had not run out. There was no last call on a required ingredient. They were his deadlines—deadlines in which he had the energy for the idea and in which his brain could create. That was his window.

Two more nights passed—the second, thankfully, with a little more sleep. His mornings had changed. He did not lie in anymore and often did not shower. On the third morning, he had coffee and a small breakfast ready in his office.

He had found it, one day earlier. It was not perfect, but it was a starting point. He had become aware of the MVP principle again. Start with a minimum viable product—something that works, though just barely, and that is enough to validate the consumer's wishes.

The idea was really simple. For centuries, enough mathematics had been known to make extensive substantive calculations based on certain data points. David simply needed those points. The great insight he had was that clothes did not have to fit perfectly from the get-go. That was his ultimate goal, but it could come later. He had to have certain key points: elbows, knees, chest, neck, and hips. He had a list of thirty-four points, half of which could be deduced from the other half.

The idea was to physically print the points on very thin fabric that someone could put on. Fabric that was tight around the body, like tights.

It would not be perfect, but it would give very reliable measurement points. And an additional advantage was that the panty points—that was the working title—were a nice marketing tool. He would simply distribute thousands of copies at the opening. There would surely be a cohort of early adopters who would take it up. They would have a fantastic experience, and things would grow from there. That would give him time to develop the tights further or wait for better technology to be developed.

This one little idea had bred a whole series of new ones. If people measured themselves by means of the points and pictures taken with the app, they could see a mannequin of themselves on the internet. They could browse clothes— for those who liked that, they could let the algorithm make suggestions based on input— but he had also come up with a new model. Or at least it was new for him. Everyone could become a stylist and open themselves up to the world, and people could give them advice. The best advisers would get superior ratings, and their hours would be rewarded with com-missions. He could even open it up to brands, which could hire stylists to market them. In fact, there were a lot of revenue models. To David, this was a really good sign.

He wanted the experience to be not only for the happy few. It had to be available glob-ally, and there also had to be choices available to lower-income geographies. The only thing one needed was a smartphone, or a phone with a camera, and the panty points. But David would hand those out for free.

People could see themselves, lo-fi, in a series of pictures based on their selection. But with a little better access to technology, they could also walk around themselves. The phone would not only function as a camera and thus as a measuring tool, but also as a self-evaluation tool. People could walk around and judge themselves just by using their smartphones.

He also had power users in mind. He had to have real fanatics. These would be the people who would inspire the rest of the world. These people needed a completely seamless virtual-reality experience. He saw it all laid out before him. You put on your glasses and walk through various choices. The item can be rotated, and all the information you need is there. You can invite friends and experts and choose clothes together in real time. Then, with a simple hand movement, you can see yourself from all angles. You can change colors and adjust knots and lengths, all in VR. David had laughed. Finally, a really useful application of virtually reality that wasn't porn or an "experience a roller coaster" gimmick.

So much had to be done, but everything gave him an energy he had not felt for years. He had already spent a sum comparable to a German sports car on domain names: fashion.com, clothing.com, and his favorite, wear.it.

Among the full A2 sheets was one that did not go to the shredder. It was a Gantt chart—blocks of time that told him exactly when to do what. He would soon start with the first parallel workflows: development of the front end, inputs for measurements and the sources for those inputs, and printing equipment for a test site.

His whole agenda was cleared for him. David knew that that was a fairly easy task. He was sure it would take his staff about thirty seconds. Surprisingly, however, after more than an hour, his staff did come back with a question.

"Sir."

"Yes?" David had reacted irritably. He was in the middle of researching 3D printable fabrics.

"Your appointments, sir."

"Yes."

"Most of your appointments have been removed. Your agenda is almost completely empty."

"Except?" David felt an *except* coming. He wanted to get back to more important things as soon as possible.

"Well, there was an appointment circled with red exclamation marks. An appointment with your father about a certain membership."

# 17. MARIA

FreeMind88. She could have kicked herself. She, Maria the Master Criminal, had accepted a bid from FreeMind88. She had risked her whole life for someone who had come up with a name like that.

She'd been too greedy. The second offer was also pretty good—lower, but still quite a tidy sum. The prospective buyer's online name looked like a common surname—a lovely, local-sounding surname.

The messages back and forth should also have been a red flag. She did not speak the language perfectly yet either, but this guy was making typos in every other word. And she'd never chatted with anyone who'd used so many numerals in his banter. The last message was "L8R."

There was no way back. They had agreed to meet at a very public place in two hours' time.

Maria would have to start heading there soon. The meeting place was as far away from her family as possible.

It felt like a drug deal, even though she was selling harmless consumer electronics. Actually, it was illicit electronics, but that was not the main concern right now.

He would pay cash.

She had typed, "Come on your own." She had later realized that this was unnecessary paranoia, but fortunately the guy had responded.

"1'll half mself dr0pped off r0nd the corner—no problem," or something along those lines, with lots of typos and strewn with needless numerals, pretty much at random.

Maria paced up and down in the living room. She was talking to herself. She had memorized a list of all the steps she had to go through. How to drive there. How she would make herself easy to spot. Where she would put the cash. How she would do her version of skedaddling if she had to.

This last bit made her especially nervous.

She had found a shopping mall with an entry and an exit. She could get to the shopping mall quite quickly and run into the car park through the stairwell.

It was a good location with a good plan B option if she needed to leave in a hurry—though she could not envision running, and she was pretty sure that even the most out-of-shape police officer would be able to catch up with her in no time.

"There's no going back now. There's no going back now. All you have to do is stop this in time, Maria—but later. It'll be worth it—really." Maria was trying to give herself some encouragement.

"Mama?"

She got such a start. She hadn't noticed, wrapped up as she was in her own little world, that her son had been watching her the whole time.

"Do you have to go to work again?"

"No . . . I mean . . . yes. But not for long. Mama will be home soon, sweetie."

"But you said you'd play tic-tac-toe with me." His disappointment hit her hard every time, even though she told herself that everything she did, she did for him.

"You're right, sweetie. You're right. I'll be back before you know it. And you know what? I'll have a new game!"

"Oh wow—really?"

"That's right—the one you pointed out to me last week, with the spaceships and the dice that have more than six faces."

"Are you going to buy it for me? Really? I don't have to wait for my birthday?"

"No, sweetie. Now don't go getting used to it, but sometimes you deserve something really special."

Maria's son didn't know what "deserve" meant, but he had already run out of the room shouting, "The spaceships and the dice! The spaceships and the dice!"

Maria had to focus again. She had a job to do, and if she did it well, it could change her life. It was already a first step in the right direction, criminality be damned.

She checked her list again. She had the right clothes on, and she knew which buses to take, both there and back. She had her special box for the money. It was waterproof, and if worst comes to worst, she could run, or at least walk fast.

She picked up the box, which was inconspicuously packed in a sturdy carrier bag from the local supermarket. She had put some of her own cash into it for the bus fare. She did not want to carry a wallet or anything else that would allow her to be identified.

This was the moment—*her* moment. She was going to be an insider. She was going to live the life of the other, native inhabitants of this country. The end justified the means.

She put on her sneakers and, unusually for her, put on a hoodie with the hood up.

"Are you leaving? Now?"

Maria heard her husband in the distance. She could hear from his voice that he had not gotten up from the sofa to check whether she was actually walking toward the front door. Maria sighed and decided to say goodbye quickly.

"I'll be right back. There's food in the fridge—two minutes in the microwave on high."

"And what about him?"

"Him? You mean your son?"

"I've been watching him all day."

"He was at school, and I was at work." Maria tried to calm herself. This was not the moment—anything but.

"So you're telling me I've gone nuts, huh?"

Maria decided not to respond. She started to head downstairs, toward her sneakers and her shopping bag.

"I'll be right back. Make sure he takes his vitamins."

"Oh, so now you're going to start telling-mewhaddadooo." It was clear by now that he'd been drinking.

"And that bag? You're going to work with that bag—at this hour?"

Maria again decided not to answer. She had to focus. She had to make sure not to waste her energy coming up with excuses, let alone arguing.

"You're nadakshley gonna go to work at all, are ya? You've gone and bought something again. Nice clothes again, huh? Or perfume. You're all the same. We're here eating leftover garbage day in, day out, while Mama's preening in front of the mirror in her fancy French dresses."

It was all Maria could do to contain herself. She bit her lip, hard. She was the only one who worked. She had been walking around in the same clothes for years, and if they did eat leftovers now and again, it was so she could at least afford a proper school lunch for her son and pay for her husband's drinking habit.

"Work, work, work. Always off somewhere, and nothing in return. You're lying! I knew it all along."

Maria could barely conceal her anger. Tears welled up in her eyes, and she bit through the skin of her lower lip.

She turned around. She had to focus; she had to get out of here. She decided to take this as a sign that she and her son needed to escape this. This was her test.

She whispered to herself, "The end justifies the means. The end … justifies … the … means."

She headed toward the front door. She quietly checked again whether she had everything with her. As she put her hand on the door handle, she heard her husband get up.

He came stomping toward her. Maria slammed the door open and scampered down the stairs, whispering the same mantra: "The end justifies the means."

She left as fast as she could. Behind her, she heard her husband's bellowing, which soon faded, however.

Maria caught a bus ten minutes earlier than she had planned. She sat down at the very back. She wiped the tears from her cheek. She could taste the blood trickling from inside her lower lip.

People looked at her, but not for too long. They clearly didn't want anything to do with her or her problems. They probably had enough problems of their own.

Maria looked at her sneakers. Through the tears, she had to chuckle to herself. At least she had gotten in some practice running.

# 18. DAVID

The man who was wearing so many layers despite the pleasant temperature laughed. He was laughing at him, but in a seemingly polite way.

"I've been working in this industry for over twenty years. Everyone is unique and wants personal treatment. I've been hearing for years that it will all end, that the internet will take over everything. Well if that's true, how come I've managed to open three new shops in the last two years?"

David couldn't stop thinking back to his first conversations with so-called restaurant experts. It was the exact same experience. These "experts" always meant well. They wanted to help this young man avoid making a big mistake by trying something that had zero chance of success.

"Machines and food do not go together. Food is an experience, and consumers know that only cooks can guarantee its high quality."

When he'd started his second financing round, he'd put that on a PowerPoint slide. The very next slide showed his growth figures. And the one after that had quotes from very satisfied, and loyal, customers. The expert turned out, after all, to be anything but.

And still, David had gone to an expert again. He knew he had to give away a hint of his idea, and he knew he would be laughed at and that the nice gentleman with all the right intentions wanted to keep him from this impending financial disaster.

But he had gone all the same, partly to learn a few things about fashion. Where could he buy it? What was selling well? When are the so-called seasons everyone's always going on about? But he'd also learned that people—especially experts—who tell you something can't be done are the best form of encouragement there is. The more people who said it was impossible and that he was crazy, the greater his determination to pull it off. It was the perfect remedy for a crisis of motivation or for when he was stuck in a project.

"But in the end, your customers just want clothes. Just as they visit a butcher for a piece of meat or an antique dealer for an antique," David said.

"Customers want so much more—that's just it. Clothing doesn't just keep you warm and protect your private parts. It gives you an identity and a way to shine."

David made a note. This was the wisest thing the man had said. He would have to do something with it. It also made him a bit sad. This insight gave him a picture of humanity that he found pitiable. So this is what humanity had come to. A certain color of jumper or a logo on a cap was needed to achieve something, whether that was status, self-confidence, or some sense of belonging. Maybe what he needed to do was not fix what was wrong with fashion but think of a means for people to gain and keep their self-confidence that did not involve this kind of theater. He thought of all those people who were already struggling to make ends meet and who spent their hard-earned cash on Italian designer clothes because it gave them the illusion of social mobility or belonging. But David decided to stick with his idea. The consumer had a need that he had to meet in a better way, and he did not have the means to transform that entire need into something else.

"And what ultimately determines what the best choice is? A brand? A color? A type of fabric? And who influences these choices?"

"Magazines, celebrities, and me—we decide, and that's what my customers rely on. People know what I stand for: impeccable advice. They know that they will walk out of my shop with what is relevant now."

"So what you're selling in particular is your authority?"

"I've never thought about it like that. But yes, maybe that's right. You can find this same garment elsewhere, including on the internet."

"But still they come back to you. Isn't the customer just being lazy?"

"No, the customer is king."

David noticed that his time was up and that he had stepped over an imaginary boundary. It was clear that the expert thought highly of his own role as a fashion moderator. He thanked the man and made a point of buying a set of cufflinks that were lying on the counter. It was nice to know at least one thing for sure: he would never wear those cufflinks.

David walked back. He'd taken a taxi to the shop, but it turned out to be just a ten-minute ride. He reflected on the conversation, which had given him more insights than he'd been expecting.

He still disagreed with the man. Of course, the whole industry could be different. There is a consumer need. There is a route to market.

There are several channels from which consumers derive value. The factory, the designer, the seller, the transporter: they all represented value—value for which a large number of consumers were willing to pay a hefty premium.

What he now thought about differently were the function of brands and the function of the people and institutions that sold them. In fact, it was not just that consumers were drawn by the primary need to stay warm by clothing themselves. They also bought their way out of insecurity. They wanted to look like somebody, to belong. Their clothes stood for things such as "I am up to date with the latest trends" or "Look at me, I really like being outdoors," or "I'm rolling in it because I've got this logo on my cap."

He had to think of a solution to this. This seemed to meet most people's needs, and it was here that the margin seemed to be. He did not want to throw away his initial idea. He still wanted to create a virtual space where people saw themselves wearing the clothes they were looking at and where they could have friends think along with them—or perhaps a computer algorithm that would select the best option based on all kinds of input. But he also needed an authority, an entity that gave consumers the confidence that its advice would help them give off the aura they were after. He also understood that consumers did not have this level of self-assurance. He couldn't come straight out and ask them, "Do you want to show your wealth through your choice of clothes?"

He was not quite there yet. But he had already received the first reward; he had energy again—an energy he had not felt for quite some time. He had another reason to get out of bed, an *ikigai*.

He'd spoken not only to experts but also to those in the know, like online department stores and online personal shoppers, so he'd gotten a really good picture. There was a lot of competition from giants that had a huge turnover and that would be hard to compete with. And that was just how David wanted it.

The conversation with the expert had made him uncertain at first. Was he on the right path? Could he really have figured out this industry so easily with just common sense? Wasn't fashion much more complex than the fast-food industry? Were people—consumers—ready for this?

But if David had learned one thing, it was that at a certain point you just have to start. First ideas are almost never the ones that make it to the end, whatever "the end" might be. David had seen so many entrepreneurs give up. Smart, talented folks with good ideas. A good hypothesis. It happened more often than not. They started out in fine spirits, but then, as soon as their brilliant idea started to seem less than brilliant, they gave up. One obstacle, one setback, and they decided that the industry just couldn't be changed. This kind of carry-on had always frustrated him to no end.

One time, he'd begun a half-hour monologue against an entrepreneur who had thrown in the towel. "What did you think? That your first idea was perfect, that it was fully thought through and spot on from start to finish? Well, of course it wasn't. You've started, and that's quite something. But you've been given what is most valuable in your journey: feedback from real consumers who are telling you what they want. That's no reason to give up the ghost. On the contrary—it's pure gold. Really direct feedback so you can iterate your idea. Look at Airbnb. Those guys started with an air-mattress concept. Air mattresses! It's a ridiculous idea of course, but they didn't let that stop them. They took their idea, left a lot of things the same, and changed a few things, again, and again, and again. Iteration is everything. Really."

David had already made his point in the first minute. But he had proceeded to give twenty other examples, all with the same purpose. All the value lay in implementing the idea and then

listening to consumers and continually making little adjustments based on their feedback.
It was so obvious, but time and again, he saw
entrepreneurs just drift off and lose focus. They
had an idea, but the consumers said they didn't
like it, so they just dropped it. The point was
to start, and then start listening and adjusting
the product or service by adding value based
on each bit of feedback. Every month, every
week—or preferably every day. Time was the
enemy, and at some point, the money would
run out, but until then, entrepreneurs had to
iterate until they dropped, sometimes literally.
That's how David saw things.

He'd been saying this for years to anyone
who would listen. And now it was time for him
to walk the talk. He hated it when experts did
not live up to their advice. He would not be
guilty of this.

He decided that there's an idea, or rather
a theme. There's a customer need. The idea is
unique and has the potential to be better for the

consumer than many of the substitutes. There was no reason to wait any longer. Phase one was done. Now phase two had to begin: implementation, listening, and iterating. Implement, listen, iterate. David repeated it to himself ten more times. His gait was shaped by the rhythm of the three words, and he was soon home.

Where to start? Would he have to go shopping for clothes? No, of course not. He could validate the idea and then fulfill the need. If anyone was going to buy anything, he could go and find the item, even if it was at a slight loss. This was still better than owning stock even before he had validated his idea.

He had to start with the consumer, with what the customer would see, with what would convince them to become a paying customer. In the end, that was what he had to determine. What could he offer that people would click on with the intention of spending money on it?

He had to think big and start with something significant. There would be expectations from the industry since he had RoboWok under his belt this time. He had to start with the ultimate user, the perfect consumer. A person, male or female, who would be willing to take his advice in an environment that would be better than any other alternative. Better than web shops, better than personal shoppers—better than shops, period.

He had already drawn it. He had first visualized it and then put it on paper. He was not good at drawing—far from it. Yet it was worth drawing to get everything from his brain down on paper. Here, too, he went through several versions.

His last version was good enough. He would target people who already had virtual-reality glasses. Virtual reality, or augmented reality, was the solution. It was like a mirror but so much better. One could see oneself from every angle, and one did not have to actually change clothes to see different options. It was so clear.

He had also figured out the entire supply chain and with it the initial marketing apparatus. Cheap tights with dots. It was not optimal, but it was a good start. This, combined with the camera on people's phones, would give a good picture of the body. He could then project this into a VR environment.

There would be several ways to manage this. They could just shop in the traditional way. It was not inspiring, but he had to have a system for every option so the consumer could just scroll down and review options. But David also felt that his first version should offer personal shopping based on input from acquaintances or from his bot. He would create an algorithm that could give advice based on various sources. He would copy the competition and use input based on social media but also from answers to subtle questions. He would also use artificial intelligence to determine whether consumers were risk-averse in making fashion choices and to figure out what was good enough to overcome their insecurities. For especially insecure consumers, he could buy rights from a celebrity that they could mimic, while for others, he could choose a more anonymous, but good-looking, avatar.

The idea was far enough along. Now he had to start building. The painful insight he had was that he could not do much. He always said that openly, and people always laughed. They thought David was being falsely modest. David knew better. He could see and think of things that others could not. He could talk to all sorts of people who actually had a craft, but he himself had hardly any real skills.

Yet he wanted to make a start wherever he could. The drawings, the calculations, the customer research—that's what everyone could do, including David. He could outsource everything, but he had to do it himself. He owed it to himself. Otherwise, what was the point? Just to make more money? To show the world that he could do it again? No, it was about creating, having a reason to live. That was the purpose—nothing else.

He knew that he could not get away from relying on developers. He had to have his vision programmed. Yet he wanted to postpone it. He wanted it to look good, and he would have to be very clear about his vision when he finally started talking to programmers.

He would write down everything, exactly what he expected from the software, without going too far. Another big lesson was not to tell specialists too much about what to build. The good ones knew what had to be done and could find the best way forward. Time after time, David had thought he had the best solution at RoboWok. But time after time, his best developers came up with better solutions. The goal they reached was the same, but the road they had taken to it was so much better.

He knew that a key last step before going to a specialist was to understand the virtual-reality part—a world almost as foreign to him as fashion. In order to have some feeling that he was making progress, he decided to spend the rest of the day understanding—or better yet, *experiencing*—the current world of VR.

He began to search. He knew he had such a device. When the money had started coming in, it was one of his first purchases, even before the house. He first tried to find it himself. Soon, his head of staff was standing in front of him. It was a title that she had come up with for herself.

"David, sir?"

David looked up, wanting to show that he was busy and did not want to talk about staff, cleaning issues, or new household purchases.

"Are you looking for something?"

Only now did David understand that he was being offered help. *Not cool, not cool,* he told himself. He did not allow himself to draw conclusions about what people thought without getting reliable information from those people themselves.

"Oh, yes, I am. It'd be great if you could help me." David reached into his pocket and grabbed his phone. He knew that VR glasses would seem too vague a description, so he Googled a picture of the device.

The head of staff looked at the picture. "I recognize the device. I'll go and investigate."

David nodded. He wanted to keep the conversation short. He knew how fleeting inspiration was. He wanted to use all his energy for the idea, his next big project, and not waste it on a conversation about the search for a device.

# 19. NATASHA

Dictionaries were also once written by people, just like encyclopedias. Nobody thinks about it, but brains, presumably male brains at the time, had spent countless hours on this. It must have felt amazing to reach words such as zeal, zebra, and zoo.

Natasha looked at the bottom of her screen. There were 120 slides. She had spent weeks of her life—her young, vital life—making 120 slides. Today it was time for slide 121. She was just over halfway.

Slides one to 120 were relatively quick and painless. She had accepted her fate, and then it was as if her brain and hands had taken over in autopilot mode. She couldn't remember much about the work. It felt like pure emptiness.

Alarm clock. Wake up. Shower. Coffee. Walk a little. Jacket off. Even more coffee.

Create slides. Lunch. Coffee. Create slides. Head home. A readymeal in the microwave. Even the films she watched in the evening were empty. She didn't have a clue what they were about, even though she had watched them all only in the last month of her life.

Slide 121 was different. The content was pretty much the same. She could probably copy over 95 percent of it from previous slides. But her brain and her hands were on strike, which she could well understand. She had had lunch and her last coffee of the day. That coffee was never worth having. What little enjoyment she got out of it did not even come close to the first two of the day.

She had already made a start twice, but after hours of staring and clicking she had deleted everything and started again with a clean slate.

She was asking the wrong questions. Why? Where does this lead? How did I fall for this? Is this my fate? Am I the weakling who sees that things can be done differently and has the chance to make that happen but stays put anyway? She was afraid that, in no time at all, she would suddenly be seventy, on her own, in a small apartment full of cats, watching TV quiz shows where she knew the answers to all the questions except those on current affairs. She would be a bitter old lady, wondering all day how different her life could have been. She had opted for financial security, but now she no longer had the energy to make use of that.

This was anything but a good day. She should have known when the shower wouldn't warm up and her coffee machine hadn't let a single drop through the filter.

Her phone vibrated. She saw on the small screen the same thing that had appeared on her computer screen. An email with an exclamation mark.

She often received emails with red exclamation marks, but this one seemed to be somewhat relevant.

The good news was that someone was actually waiting for her work. The bad news was that he needed it tomorrow. It had to be done and dusted and on his desk in twelve copies with a nice plastic cover.

Natasha felt something that she used to feel every day in the early days of RoboWok: an uneasy mix of panic, adrenaline, and a crazy tingling in her forehead, legs, and hands.

She used to love it. At least she had learned to appreciate it. It meant that something had to be done, that she was the only one who could do it, and that if she succeeded, she would have contributed to her higher calling: healthy food—and thus healthier lives—for all.

That feeling was gone. It was the same panic but without the prospect of the payoff. She realized this almost immediately and resented it.

She opened the slide and slapped her right cheek with the flat of her hand. "Come on now," she said to herself.

For a while, this seemed to make her productive and lead to an hourly output that would enable her to meet her deadline. But the effect was short-lived.

Halfway through the slide, there was a box that looked like other boxes on previous slides. Her adrenaline was replaced with emptiness—or maybe something even less.

And once again she had the same questions. Why? Where does this lead? She had a new vision of her seventy-year-old self, surrounded only by cats.

The hours flew by. Her body stayed put except for a few moments when she went to get more coffee. She had gone way over her coffee quota. In the meantime, she had turned to a number of second-order tasks—making a front cover and getting a start on a table of contents. She had also set everything in one font of the same size. Titles were consistent, and she had made a few small edits to earlier slides. But all the slides after number 120 were empty.

She kept egging herself on. But the emptiness won out. She stood up and looked around. The office was empty. In the distance, there was a lamp with a bulb that was flickering its last and two screens that had been left on. One of them had a screensaver of a little man peeing on the Microsoft Windows logo. Funnily enough, the computer belonged to a guy who had spent his whole life working with Microsoft software, including Windows.

Her gaze moved from the lamp to the screensaver and then back to the empty slide on her screen. The emptiness had now truly won the day. She grabbed her coat. Normally she would have shut down her computer and turned off the monitor, cleared away the empty cups on her desk, and even wiped away the coffee rings with a cloth. But not this time.

She headed out the door and took the elevator. Without her having to look, her index finger found the floor that had the back entrance through the car park where there were cars of mostly white men who actually came by car, which seemed very impractical to her in this crowded, built-up city.

The elevator doors opened, and instead of going left as she usually did, she now walked right and into the car park. She left it on a road that was reserved for cars and overconfident cyclists. She waited for two taxis to pass and then crossed the street, heading toward the worst part of town, as it was called. She had always found it strange that that was what it was called. The food there was tastier and more affordable. The only downside was that it was not served on oversized plates. The buildings were lower, and the brickwork was more charming. However, there always seemed to be garbage bags by the doors, as if people wanted to be ready for the garbage truck a week ahead of time.

The people who were on the streets at this time seemed either to be in a hurry or to be pan-handling. Natasha was the only one who was wandering around quietly without a purpose.

She walked through this neighborhood and then on to the next one without a thought. This was a neighborhood that people talked about and which no one she knew had ever been to. She had been walking through it for some time, and it was only when she was halfway through it that she realized it actually wasn't so bad at all. In fact, there was little difference between it and the first one she had come through.

She had been walking for quite some time in shoes that were really not meant for this. However, she felt no pain, and her legs would not stop. It was as if her legs were helping her brain. They had to keep at it to give her brain, which was processing a large amount of information, time to think.

In the meantime, she had ended up in a neighborhood that felt much less urban. There were many more cars, most of them quite large. There was nobody on the street. At first, she had seen an elderly woman looking at her through the blinds of her living room. It seemed as if her passing was the most startling thing in the woman's day, or perhaps even in her entire week.

Now she began to feel her feet. The pain came on, not gradually, but in an instant. Despite the pain, she walked on until she came to a really small park with a playground that also boasted a lot of garbage cans.

She found the only bench in the park and sat down. She took off her left shoe—most of the pain was in her left foot today—and saw the devastation underneath. Tears welled up in her eyes, and she found herself crying. She soon realized she was crying, not from the pain, but from stress—from her work, but especially from her life. What had happened? How had she ended up here? Did she not deserve better? Surely the idea was that if you worked hard at something good, karma would reward you.

She wasn't naïve. She understood that things didn't happen just like that. She had to work for it and be patient. Do the right things. Don't drink too much. Don't gamble. Help your neighbors. Pay your taxes and do what your boss asks of you. The problem, however, was that she no longer had confidence in the end goal. What would this lead to—a promotion? And if it did, would everything suddenly be fun? Would the extra few bucks a month open some magical doors to happiness?

The professional goals, the extra pay, the social status—it was all quite meaningless in the end. Why hadn't she seen this before? She could have saved herself all this bother by thinking about it earlier. Or was it that she had to go through this in order to get to this understanding?

Things had to be different, but she had realized that long ago. Then what was she still doing here? Why was the rhythm of her life the way it was? Why was she spending her time the way she was? The goal had disappeared. There was no longer any reason for the path to something that no longer existed.

In the distance, she saw a needlessly large car. She wiped away her tears and hid behind a sign. Fortunately, the car drove past. She looked at it carefully as it passed. She had to chuckle through her tears at the number plate: 2BIG4ME2.

# 20. BERNARD

Cufflinks—check. Hair—check. Button closed, button open—check.

Bernard did not want to take any risks. He did not want his looks to get in the way of his considerable intellect. Before entering the main hall, he stood in front of the mirror and decided he was presentable.

He was late, which hardly ever happened. The session had already begun.

The agenda had been sent out earlier that week, and that was when he had decided to show up late.

It was actually not the done thing. Normally the members drank together and then ate together. A modular approach wasn't really an option; you were either all-in or not in at all.

Yet there had been a meeting years before that had stuck in Bernard's mind. It was about an extension to the building that had been talked about for years. People constantly disagreed, and it was not as if there were just two different thoughts. There were five or so different approaches, each of which had a significant constituency.

That evening—it was about four or five years before, as he recalled—was the moment for the big vote to be held. It was decided—and this was a major exception—that no one idea had to command a majority. Any idea with just one vote more than the others, even if it was supported by only 21 percent, say, of the voters, would be chosen.

The evening had started early. The meal was eaten relatively quietly and was over relatively quickly. Even the drink after the meal— normally almost everyone's favorite part—was over much faster. The meeting had started. One by one, people were allowed to speak one more time. One spoke passionately about preserving architecture, while another wanted to optimize light. One fairly small group wanted to call the whole thing off. They were all strong presentations, and all were well prepared. They were all received with a relatively loud, "Hear! Hear!" though there was never any clapping at the club—except for a guest artist, and then mostly by slapping a hand on a thigh, while the other hand held a glass or something to smoke.

Strangely enough, the gentlemen had to wait for the final presentation. Stranger yet, the speaker, normally one of the most authoritative members on almost any subject, was not there. People were worried about his health, which was not surprising given his age and his drinking habits. They had tried to call him, but to no avail.

Just as the chairman of the day was about to give the presentation to someone else in the man's camp—which actually meant that the voting could begin—the old wooden door creaked open.

"Do you hear that, gentlemen? Not only the doors, but also the acoustics! The smell, the feel of the wood, the cracks that run along the walls and ceilings. This is all meant to be. This is the origin and the foundation of all that we have. This would not have been the case if the place had continually been renovated. It should not be tampered with. It should be adjusted as little as possible. The smallest difference can change the energy it emanates. Look at this mirror. It has been hanging ever so slightly crooked—about four degrees off, I'd say—since the beginning. Don't even think about using a spirit level. That would be the last straw—the difference between what we have around us now and what we used to have."

The room broke its silence as men consulted among themselves. One of them—one of the oldest members for an opposing camp— called out over the whispered consultations, "Well, thanks at least for the untimely—or timely—entrance. Great bit of theatrics there. I'll give you that."

The whole room, even the last presenter's own camp, found this riposte rather amusing. The waiters showed no change in emotion.

"Apologies, gentlemen. A bit of theatre. A bit of suspense. Whatever is needed for the greater good. Leave it. Leave it as it is. The grounds are large enough. Yes, we need more space, but a standalone building is the better idea!"

Not much later, the voting took place. The idea the man had just pushed for won out more easily than had been expected.

Bernard had not forgotten the entrance, the speech, and especially the effect. He had been intending to use this trick for years. He understood that it was plagiarism and that the effect might be diminished by now. Still, that was a few years ago, and no one had repeated it since. And besides, the goal he had in mind was much less drastic, and he would do it only the once—make a late entrance, that is.

Bernard had the agenda for the evening in his pocket. He looked at it again. The evening would start with financial accounts and a small presentation about their outing, which he had not been on. He had not gone because the cathedral they had gone to, which was far away, was of no interest to him. Why would he want to see a presentation on it?

He was concerned with the third point on the agenda for the evening: "rejuvenation." It was the most important agenda item for years—the most important, in fact, since the construction of the country house. More space had been built, but ironically, the membership had only shrunk since then. Many drawers were no longer in use, and in recent years, the growth had been quite meager. Things had come to such a pass that men were admitted who had had no chance before—even one who had not finished university. It had been a scandal, even though within a few months the man had earned his stripes.

This was his topic. He had to manage it. It was he who had nominated the youngest member for a decade—his very own son. He had the keys to the new generation, the new captains of industry, the men who were worthy of joining the club.

Bernard held his left ear to the door. His right ear had virtually no function anymore, except to ensure the symmetry of his head. He waited patiently for point three to start. Twice he had been startled when a member of staff opened the door unexpectedly, and twice he had quickly run into the cloakroom—at least his version of running. Bernard told himself that nobody had seen him.

The presentation on the cathedral had come to an end. This was his moment. In the distance, he heard the chairman of the day say, "Gentlemen, let us now turn to the main topic of the evening—the first important step in securing the next one hundred years of this splendid club."

He heard the audience murmuring quietly in agreement.

"If we don't intervene now and keep going the way we're going, it will be empty here in ten years' time."

"And we must not allow that to happen!" Bernard walked in somewhat awkwardly in an attempt to theatrically take over the point.

Most of the men—those who could physically do it—turned around and looked at Bernard in amazement.

Bernard took a note from his breast pocket. He had practiced it several times at home in front of the mirror, but with the current pressure, he needed his notes. It took quite a long time. The theatrical moment morphed slowly into an embarrassing one. Fortunately, the chairman of the day had enough empathy to allow Bernard his moment. In the hall, a number of men had already given up.

"Gentlemen," he began, without having realized there was an issue. He was still in his own zone. It was his moment, which he had prepared down to the last detail. He thought that everything was going according to plan and that the men in the audience were hanging on his every word.

"We all know it; there are only two certainties in life."

"Death and taxes," two men shouted almost in sync.

"That's it indeed." Bernard did not appreciate the interruption but decided to continue. He repeated, "Death and taxes." The repetition was not necessary, but it was in his notes.

"We too, no matter how vital we feel, will one day be no more. The world is changing rapidly, and the generations that have followed us are different. They have different norms—different values. Technology is accelerating, and the classes are blurring one into the other."

Everyone tried not to look at the man who had not been to college. People avoided looking at him so much that it became clear that it was precisely him that everyone was thinking about.

"But what we have here, gentlemen, is something for the ages."

Bernard actually had the audience with him to some extent. It was no Martin Luther King Jr. moment, but apparently it resonated enough with those present.

Bernard found his stride and pressed on with more confidence than he'd started with.

"In a world of golden hubcaps and access for all to media—where a folk musician of all people can win the Nobel Prize in Literature."

The audience actually laughed. Perhaps for the first time in his life, Bernard had made a room full of men laugh. It wasn't meant as a joke. These were observations that he had written down seriously, in all earnestness. But he seized his moment and laughed with the room as if the joke had been carefully planned all along.

"What we have must be protected—preserved for future generations. Everything changes, but not this need. The need to have a place with like-minded people. Men with similar interests, men who have made something of themselves. Men who know what it is all about."

"Cognac!" The room fairly exploded in uproarious laughter. Over it, someone in the back called out, "Good one!" And nearer the front: "Oh, just priceless!"

The wiseacre, whom Bernard did not immediately recognize, was now the one getting the laughs. This wasn't some second-rate comedy club. Bernard had to regain the initiative. It was an important point—in fact, the only one that really mattered.

"Gentlemen. Gentlemen—please."

It took a while before he had the room back. A young waiter offered him a glass of water. It was perfect timing. Bernard decided to give the boy a nod.

The quiet had returned, and the audience actually looked at Bernard. He had the room again. He knew it had to happen now. He took a sip of water.

"Gentlemen. This is serious business. The survival of this institution is at stake. I know I am not alone, yet I feel that this is my higher purpose, my legacy. I have lived a life of great achievements, but this feels like my primary legacy. Let me build the bridge. Let me find the new generation. Let me fill these rooms again with young men, young men who will also find their like-mindedness and find the enrichment that I have found here. I offer myself, all my remaining days. Let me be the bridge builder."

Bernard quickly looked at his cheat sheet.

"Let me be the bridge builder!" The note clearly stated in all caps: "REPEAT SENTENCE."

Bernard was now expecting a standing ovation. Men who would slap his shoulders. Here and there a heartfelt "Bravo-o-o!"

There was none of that. Just silence, with quiet murmur here and there. It was a most uncomfortable minute for Bernard. He took his time to find a seat somewhere. He had waited a long time for his moment at the door, and his legs now clearly indicated that enough had been done.

Bernard was lucky with the chairman of the day, to put it mildly. He was a very empathetic man who understood what this meant for Bernard. He understood how Bernard had experienced the moment. He broke the long silence. The murmuring stopped.

"Let us vote. I will start. You have my vote." The chairman of the day held up his right hand and nodded kindly to Bernard. Bernard was relieved and decided to send the chairman a letter of thanks with a good bottle of wine later. He made a note to himself to get something inexpensive from the supermarket that didn't *look* like plonk.

Quietly, more hands went up. One by one, Bernard counted the hands. He estimated that there were just under thirty men present. A show of sixteen hands should be enough.

It took a while, and every extra hand felt very good. The moment between one hand and the next felt like an eternity.

Bernard counted twelve hands. And then to make things even more tense, the chairman of the day asked, "Is anyone else offering to play this role?"

Bernard decided then and there to drop the idea of the thank you letter and the bottle of wine. From one moment to the next, the friendly chairman of the day had become a Judas in his eyes.

Another minute passed. It was a miracle. No one volunteered.

After a minute, the chairman broke the silence.

"Last chance."

Another minute, an eternal minute. Bernard saw the men talking to each other. A few more hands went up, slowly. Bernard counted the magic number he needed: sixteen. Most of the room still seemed to be completely unconcerned with the situation. They laughed together and drank their drinks from thick glasses.

"Once, twice . . . It is hereby decided. We have our bridge builder."

The audience actually laughed. It was unclear why people were laughing in front of Bernard. It didn't matter. He was euphoric. He stood up and bowed to the audience.

"I will reward your trust."

Some men gave a loud thump on the old tables in front of them. In the distance, there was even a "Bravo." It was one of the happiest moments in Bernard's recent life.

Bernard repeated, "I will reward your trust. And the first sign of that will soon follow. My son, David."

The audience had made itself heard. A couple of other men said, "Bravo." The evening could not be spoiled. Bernard's euphoria lasted for another two minutes. Unfortunately, the minutes seemed much shorter now.

The chairman broke the euphoria. He could really forget about the bottle of wine now.

"Gentlemen, gentlemen. The next item, the annual St. Matthew's Passion."

As far as Bernard was concerned, the audience had quickly forgotten the historic moment. The focus was on the next item on the agenda. But that didn't matter. Bernard sat alone at his little table, reflecting on his moment. They could never take this away from him.

# 21. DAVID

David unthinkingly bounced a stress ball against the wall. He was sitting in the room next to what was to be his favorite room. He had an office furnished with a worktable, large custom-made mahogany cupboards, and a desk larger than a one-person convertible. Next to the large office space, a printer room had been built. The printer had never been put in, but there was a much smaller desk, which in the end was used the most.

He had found the stress ball in a corner among other things he had been given but had never used. The stress ball had made him think. Who uses this kind of thing? What a crazy thought, that people think squeezing a ball that's too soft for any serious sport can reduce stress. Meanwhile, he had been sitting zen-like for quite some time, with the ball in his hand and virtually nothing on his mind.

To the rhythm of a slow heartbeat, he threw the ball against the wall. The wall was wonderfully white and empty, unlike all the walls hung with art and other decorations throughout the rest of his house. On the left was his laptop, on which he had open a number of websites of future competitors, but most of the screen was taken up by a spreadsheet.

David had begun to build. He had already written to a number of developers and sourced some early items to sell. Still, he had gone back to his numbers to check his business case the night before. When he started his first business, even before RoboWok, he had resolved to always calculate whether his vision could actually be realized at scale.

It was quite simple—the spreadsheet suggested calculations that were much more complex than those that had actually been done. He first calculated the possible turnover per month for the next five years. What did he sell, at what average price per unit, and at what volume per unit per month? The volume, or quantity, he called Q. He made Q so that he could play with it to see how his model would look if growth were larger or smaller, faster or slower. He had Q depend on marketing and its effectiveness.

He checked the turnover against available figures in the market—the turnover of large players—and against figures on population and spending patterns. It all seemed to portend well.

Then he started with all the variable costs. The costs that would move along with Q for the most part. From top to bottom, he started with VAT, production costs, shipping, and packaging. It was a substantial list.

When he had finished modeling the variable costs, he started on the fixed costs. Here he wanted to be complete but as conservative as possible. Checking all this was simple. Turnover minus all variable costs—his total absolute contribution margin—had to be more than all the fixed costs at scale. Then there would be profit—his definition of success. He would also have to make some investments and write off a few things. This he more or less disregarded. The return on investment on this was his happiness, his *raison d'être*.

He had played with the model for hours. He had assumed that more and more people would come to him organically—that is, that he would not have to spend marketing money on every customer. He made significant assumptions about procurement costs that would drop significantly with scale, as well as marketing effectiveness that would grow with time.

However, no matter what he tried, as long as he put in assumptions he actually believed in, the EBITDA was negative. In other words, turnover minus variable costs minus fixed costs came out negative. He had found ways to make the number come out just about in the black, but he did not believe in the assumptions he had to make in order to make that happen.

He was OK with having a Jeff Bezos mindset. Just as with Amazon, it was fine if he suffered losses for years and years—he could take it and he would be happy to. But, at least on paper, it would eventually have to be a profitable operation at scale, not a prestige project he would have to keep throwing money at until the end of time.

For a moment, he considered taking the plunge. He would be able to spend the rest of his life making up for the losses he generated. But something was stopping him. It was a principle. He wanted to be the person who could build another company and be proud of more than just sales growth. The whole thing would have to be right. This meant that, with time, the massive turnover would have to yield a profit.

And then there was the "understanding comes naturally" phase. He just had to start, take a few years of losses, and then the insights would come. That magic way to make it a profitable business. He did not know the industry at all. Perhaps there were volume discounts he did not yet know about or enormous advantages to insourcing certain steps in the value chain. Or perhaps, like the French and Italians, he could charge ridiculous prices with time and thus make a profit with high gross margins. He did not want that. He did not think this was disruption. He wanted do things the Henry Ford way—he wanted to give more people a better experience within any budget. He refused to be that person who would sell overpriced stuff to people who could not afford it. They would end up with the problems while he reaped the profits. That was not him, and he resolved that it never would be.

The biggest problem he had encountered was that something was missing. Earlier, when he started working on such spreadsheets, he got energy, a lot of energy, from the possible profits. In this case, not only were the theoretical profits lacking, but even when he forced assumptions that got him into the black, he did not feel any real excitement. That feeling was missing.

He wanted to be above the money. He had the luxury of working on other things, of drawing energy from new sources. But still, the prospect of profits had always been his fuel. It had given him a measurable goal—something he could track daily to see whether he was on the right path, both in his professional life and in his life as a whole.

Now money was meaningless. A few months earlier, he had made a lot of money on the stock exchange. He had looked at the percentages. They were big numbers, very big numbers. But it did not do anything for him. It was as if someone had stuck a hot, thick needle into the bottom of his foot, but the rest of his body had not reacted.

His wealth had reached such a point that whatever extra amounts he earned had no effect. He already had everything. He had long since reached the point where there was nothing left that he necessarily wanted to own. In fact, things had reached a point where any pressure he felt was no longer worth it. The fortune had made him feel obliged to do something great. He owed it to billions of people to live their dream. He recalled the story of a Dutch goalkeeper who had bought a simple Volkswagen even though he had a contract worth millions with an English football club. The football fans were angry: "Our club pays you millions. You have to enjoy it. At least get a Bentley!"

Yes, he could give it all away to charity. And, in fact, he was already giving a lot to a lot of charities, but they had made him cynical. A lot of what he gave went to the government, and it seemed that none of his projects made any difference over the long term. He also wanted to keep the option of doing something great in his life. And then, when he died, everything would go to funds for the poor, for education, for girls in the poorest parts of Ethiopia. He had

had an overpaid estate-planning attorney make it official a good while back.

How could he get his mojo back? Profit was no longer about making money. It was the indicator that he had done it again—that he had generated structural revenue from nothing, and that it was a self-funding activity. That was the goal, and this new idea never seemed to reach it, despite inordinately high revenue levels.

He had gone through a series of hundreds of successful throw-catch cycles. Now the stress ball fell out of his hands. There was a knock on the door. It was strange that the ball had fallen before the knock, not after the knock, as if he were telepathic.

David got up and walked toward the door. He paid an army of people to work around his house. Nevertheless, he sprinted toward the door so as not to keep his people waiting in their scarce time on this earth.

"We have her." The head of staff was smiling. He repeated the news. "We've got her!"

David tried to make a joke. "Osama bin Laden was already caught years ago. And he's also a man, by the way."

The head of staff did not seem to appreciate the joke, or to know who this "Osama person" was. David found that difficult to understand, if it was true. There were certain news items that even non-newspaper-reading, non-news-watching people surely couldn't miss.

"No. The thief who stole your glasses."

"My glasses?"

"Your computer glasses?"

"Oh! My VR glasses." That spot in David's long-term memory went on again. Everything came back to him. "You should have become a detective."

This time, the head of staff did smile. David had never seen her smile before. Perhaps this was really her calling. And he felt called to push her toward her passion—to deliver a monologue about how short life was and to tell her that, if she wanted to be a detective, she should go for that, the challenges notwithstanding. But he kept mum. The head of staff clearly wanted to get to the point.

"We checked all the images and caught her red-handed."

Together they walked toward a room that David had forgotten was even there. Once he arrived, he saw a chair in front of a display four screens wide and three high. David found it hard to believe he had not known that these twelve monitors were in his own house.

"So watch closely. First she moves the stuff.

The team, which was supposed to clean up, had apparently all become detectives and had compiled footage of this woman. David saw how she looked around—moved all kinds of things and then made notes.

"Now here we see her a few weeks later. See that?"

"See what?"

Three men tried to push the same button. The smallest one won. The footage was rewound and then paused.

David saw his VR glasses. Someone pressed pause again, and the video played once more. He saw the VR glasses disappear into a box and then, on another screen, into another box next to a back door.

The self-appointed team of detectives, formerly cleaning staff, gave each other high fives. David congratulated them, reluctantly.

"Shall I inform the police? My apologies. I should have done this a long time ago, of course. Sorry to be bothering you with this."

"No, no. Not the police. Let me think a moment." David hurried out the door. Behind them, the team was surprised, as if they had already gotten the handcuffs ready and were disappointed not to be allowed to clip them onto the suspect.

He really did not want this kind of negativity in his life right now. He did not know, or even recognize, a lot of his staff. But he had seen this woman before. She seemed to be a hard worker. He remembered her face well. It was as if her eyes had lived three times as long as the rest of her body. She had many worries, and she worked hard. That was clear to him from the first time she had seen her.

But theft? Really? He was a good employer after all. He had no choice. He could not allow this. If he put up with this, then before he knew it, there'd be an army of trucks he'd never seen before lining up outside his door. The entire staff would be loading up his stuff. He had to intervene and show that this was not accepted. He had to send out a signal with the threat of police.

What a rotten business. He would nip further crime in the bud, but in the meantime, he'd be destroying a life, and he'd feel guilty for a long time. He could buy those VR glasses again. For her, those glasses probably meant she was able to afford things to keep herself alive. For all he knew, this could be her only way of keeping her family safe and sound.

David walked to his garage. His other garage. There was an empty space for the cars he would have to buy one day. And there was one for bicycles. He pressed a button, and the garage door opened smoothly with a quiet humming sound. David waited impatiently and then ducked under the door as soon as it was half-open. He was dressed quite warmly—wearing more than he usually did. Not just a bathrobe, shorts, and slippers. But other than the clothes on his back, he just took a bicycle. No wallet and no phone. It had been a long time since David had left his house without taking a phone.

He mounted the bike and cycled on and on, just like Forrest Gump, without any particular purpose. There was no destination and no plan. He had always wondered how, in the Tom Hanks film, the main character had not gotten tired. You never saw him eating or sleeping in between. You just saw him running and watched as his beard grew longer and longer.

He just kept on cycling. It was effortless. His legs moved without needing guidance, in a kind of perpetual motion.

# 22. NATASHA

"Young lady, do you want me to call someone? Your father? Your mother?"

Natasha was flitting from one emotion to another. Did this woman know that she was a working woman who had been away from home for years? How sweet that such an old lady would take the time to check on her. And what a compliment that she saw her as a teenager.

"No, thanks very much. I live right nearby."

It was clear from her reaction that the old lady did not believe her. The lady walked on. That made Natasha think. What would her goal be at this age? Is it purely a countdown, a waste of time? How would she look back on her life? Would she be proud of all the years she had suffered in order to be able to walk around carefree now? Or would she regret not having done everything she'd wanted to? She would probably laugh at Natasha's situation. She would laugh off the work stress, but she would probably also laugh off the trip around the world too.

She was still sitting on the same bench. Her feet still hurt. Her phone battery still had a surprising amount of power left, even though she had started working on flight tickets again.

She knew the important places she had to see. That was no longer what she was focusing on. The route and sometimes the order were less important. She had scoured all kinds of blogs for tips and tricks on finding cheaper tickets, such as taking an indirect flight to an unpopular faraway destination and then staying at the first stop instead of flying on, changing airports in big cities with multiple airports, or booking returns with many months in between. She had tried everything. There were small moments of jubilation, but the savings were often in the tens of euros, not hundreds, let alone thousands. That's is what she needed in terms of budget but also as a leg up.

As she searched for tickets, three work reminders came up—one from a colleague and two from herself. She had been setting reminders for herself for years. They had kept her productive, but now they had a completely different effect. Every work-related message had an effect on her body. It shot into her shoulders or her thighs. Often she would squeeze her eyes shut and face the heavens.

The third time, which followed shortly after the second message, it was all she could do not to throw her phone into the wet grass. Fortunately, the other side of her brain knew that that phone was also the gateway to her plane tickets.

Enough was enough. The work. She had been walking around with it for so long. She had been unhappy for months. Her rare moments of happiness did not come from going to a party or eating a nicely decorated cupcake. They came, as had happened a few times already, early in the morning when she was not yet thinking about work.

It was not even the fact of there being more work. It was that work was a major part of her life. She had started to look at it differently. The point of working used to be primarily to earn money, or at least to avoid major financial worries. But then, soon after, it became about much more. It had to be something she wanted to belong to, something she wanted to build on—something she could proudly talk about in the years ahead when she was an old lady in a park talking to twenty-somethings like herself.

She wanted more than just to build—she wanted to help produce something of value. She had to feel at home in the midst of it all. There had to be a group of like-minded people who knew what did and, especially, what did not matter.

It was clear that this did not matter. She had known that for so long, but now she was mentally ready to put it behind her. That deadline was the last straw. She thought about saying her goodbyes.

But how to do that? She refused to leave with a lot of rancor and give her colleagues the proverbial middle finger. They were people too. They had just become the way they were. She was simply wired differently, and there was nothing anyone could do about it.

But she also had to make something meaningful out of these years, in the hopes that her work would be worth something or perhaps that she would become a significant figure in the life of her far-too-inexperienced boss. Perhaps she was a kind of talisman, someone on his path who would give him an important life lesson. She had to laugh about this herself. Such self-aggrandizement! Still, she embraced the thought.

She slid open her phone with conviction. Several plane-ticket websites were already open in different apps. They showed frightening total prices. She then opened her work email.

Something had happened. Opening her work email felt very different. In fact, it felt like nothing at all. All those unread emails, which used to turn her into an adrenaline-driven hamster on a wheel, now left her completely unmoved.

She was looking for the latest version of her life's work. She could even laugh at that thought: "life's work." She found it. She pressed "forward" without feeling anything.

And then she stopped. She knew that there was a good chance that the words she would choose would end her career, or at least this career, immediately. She hesitated. The smile disappeared, and she looked around in a panic. It was dark, and there was no one around. There was no movement, except for the struggles of a thin, white plastic bag a short distance off. One handle was snagged on the branch of a big log, even as part of it was swirling unevenly in a small eddy.

She returned her gaze to her phone. She opened the file—her "life's work." She needed only one last look, and that would be it for good.

She decided to keep it short. She pressed "forward" again and typed, "Good luck tomorrow and in the years to come. C YA. Nat."

"C YA" was probably out of place, but it still worked a treat. "See ya!" It hinted unmistakably that she was done with all this. But with this casual abbreviation, she made clear that everything was OK. She was beyond the point at which they could entice her back.

Her "life's work" was incomplete. That was now his problem. And that, too, was OK. Nat had decided to be his talisman. For a moment, she thought about adding, "Oh, and don't mention it." Instead, she simply clicked "send."

# 23. MARIA

She needed her sleep so badly. The time she was given to sleep was always very limited. Still, she had been lying awake for hours. What had she done?

She had sold her stolen treasure. It seemed her plan had succeeded. FreeMind88 turned out to be a pimply-faced teenager. He certainly wasn't born in 1988. She hadn't asked what the eighty-eight stood for. That was out of character for the situation and for a master criminal.

The transfer was very underwhelming. She had thought of a much more intimidating situation. A kind of drug deal with men wearing black-hooded sweatshirts, both hands adorned with knuckle dusters. She could get used to this kind of transfer. If she did it five or six more times, it would feel completely normal. That was not the problem.

The thing that kept her awake was the process she had had to go through before. She was going through her steps. Steps she had thought up and been so proud of. She had first carefully moved objects of value and thus been able to check whether anyone would notice. If they did, she could be the hero. She could find it. Nobody knew that it had been moved for a reason.

But had she given it enough time? She had moved things around and taken them home just a few weeks later. What if he needed them just a little later? Even then, a search would be done. He had not looked at them for years. What difference would a week make to him? In any scenario, a week for him would be less painful than any week in her current life.

She was particularly angry about that. A boy, really, barely a man, who owned so much—so many things that he had no idea what he actually owned. She cherished every possession, and every purchase had to be weighed against every other expense: new clothes for her son, a hat for herself without holes to make the trip to work more bearable, a new cooker with all the burners working, or a fan to help her son sleep better during the hot summer nights.

Did her boss know about this? Would he think about this every time he clicked "Buy now" on the internet? It was a bizarre thought. Of all the times he clicked "Buy now," how many times would he then be aware of the purchase? Her hypothesis was that an hour after he'd been online clicking "Buy now," he would remember no more than five of the items he'd bought.

She knew that there were rich people in the world who were far worse. Her boss seemed nice enough, and he was good to his staff. He had to do something with all that money. What would she do in his shoes?

No, this was about the whole system. What had started with the exchange of camels for donkeys was now a system that created far too much inequality. She knew that he paid far more than most people ever would in taxes but also that it was a similar percentage. She had read that there were all sorts of tricks that could be played with income from assets versus income from salary so that less would be due in taxes. The rich got richer, so they could buy even more things they didn't need. She'd had to do it. No two ways about it.

Still, what a risk she'd been taking. Taking things from him would not hurt him. He could replace everything in his house painlessly. But still, if she were to be caught, he would have no choice but to dismiss her. He couldn't allow theft. And there were countless people out there who would give their eyes or teeth for her job. And worse yet, that would make it many times more difficult to find a new source of income. What was her plan B? Go back home? Find another job? Go to another part of the country where the cost of living was lower? It was entirely possible that her reputation would follow her everywhere and that, wherever she went, there would be much less work to be found.

She had once walked past a job fair a few streets away. That was something new for her. Mostly white boys and girls in their early twenties were walking past stalls of employers who were selling themselves to them.

"Come work for us—it'll be fun! And we'll cover your dental! Every five years, you'll get an extra month's paid holidays!"

"No, no. Come work with us. We're a people company, so our people come first. And with us, you'll earn more, and your growth path will be much more interesting."

"No—join us! We have people in our DNA! AND you'll get this mug to take home with you today."

There was a whole nother world so close to home—a world where boys and girls who had the right pieces of paper, or rather who came from "good homes," whatever *that* meant, were begged by employers to choose them.

Outside the fair, she had heard two girls talking about how much stress they felt with all those choices. Weighing up the conditions at work, the substance of the work they would be doing, and especially what it all meant. One of them wanted to work not only to make money but also to make the world a better place.

Maria took a deep sigh. It was so deep that she found even herself a little too theatrical. Some things she could make peace with. She did not have that education. The employers would choose, and getting chosen meant that a piece of paper like that would be worth a lot. She even understood that certain skills and attributes were rewarded better than others. But above all, the number of choices bothered her. She felt constrained by only one other choice: a temporary life of crime. It offered returns that were many times lower than what a future captain of industry would earn, but it entailed risks that were far greater than the fallout from flunking an exam or making a bad career move.

In any case, she'd already made the choice. There was no going back now. She had stolen and made money from it. She was a thief. The choice had now become whether she wanted to be a petty thief or a master criminal.

The term "master criminal" had become much less appealing. She no longer wanted that. That first transaction had not tasted like more. She didn't feel comfortable in her own skin, and the money felt dirty in her hands. What she bought with it would always feel dirty. She decided to use it to make repayments and not to buy anything. Anything she bought would only be a painful reminder of what she had done.

# 24. DAVID

He could have gone on cycling for ages. His legs showed no sign of fatigue.

But then—how could this happen? This was probably the most expensive bicycle one could buy on the free market at the moment, and it had never been used. Yet there he was, with a flat tire.

He had, meanwhile, gotten over the fact that price and exclusivity are not always good predictors of quality. He understood that this company had not committed to quality, or at least simple quality control. They had focused on building a brand and maximizing brand equity. Millions spent on commercials made by hip men and women with black turtlenecks and Elton John glasses.

It was a giant industry. There was a demand for these types of bicycle, and he'd fallen for it.

And not only him, but probably the manufacturer too. He saw before him a technical genius who had spent years creating the Ultimate Bicycle. The mistake he'd made was hiring "consultants"—boys and girls with an MBA (the most overvalued piece of paper in the world) who had told him not to put his resources into enhancing the actual bike but to put all the funds he raised into advertising.

He had gotten over the flat tire. But the much greater frustration now was that he was outside the area that was served by taxis. That surprised him. It seemed quite urban, at least with a high density of people who were, moreover, well heeled enough to take taxis regularly.

To calm himself, he calculated in his head how many taxis there would have to be per person on average in order for the taxi companies to break even. He calculated it in several ways. In all scenarios, this would be a great place for a taxi service. And more to the point, he had taken taxis many times in places far less suitable.

There was a combination lock on the bike. That surprised him. He did not consider himself the type to have a combination lock. He wasn't a key guy either, but knowing himself, he would have chosen a much more futuristic solution, such as a lock that was built into the bicycle and that he could open with his phone. David wanted to be able to do everything with his phone: pay, open doors, and book transport. His whole house was built for it. Today was one of those days—no transport and an old-fashioned combination lock.

He was not familiar with the combination lock. He used it as a kind of rope and with great difficulty tied this expensive bike to a tree that was way too small. It was either going to be some bike thief's lucky day, or he would sort everything out later.

He started to walk and soon realized that he actually preferred walking to cycling. All those devices. This direct contact felt much better. The pace was also more suited to his mental state. He could walk without thinking of the act of walking. As he'd cycled, he'd had to concentrate on operating the bike. He had to process a lot of information and reevaluate what was important. He had to structure it into containers, or rather group it into cohorts of similar information—and he didn't want to be distracted by riding a bike.

On his way, he came across a shop with French baked goods and nice coffee. He paid the owner by logging into PayPal via his very old PC. It actually worked—he could live without his phone. His little episode of bad luck on several fronts seemed to be over.

He drank the coffee and ate a nice round sultana roll, and for a moment, he thought of nothing in particular. His feet seemed to keep on walking on their own. Without thinking, he went into a small, empty park, where he would normally expect to find a parking lot or a public building of some kind.

He saw someone sitting on a bench. She caught his eye. She did not seem like the type he would expect to find alone on a bench in a place like this at this hour. She had one shoe, and the other was lying next to her with the sole facing upwards.

He kept his distance. He was not looking for contact. He did not need to talk to a stranger. There was work to be done. He had to make up his mind about the bungling thief. He had to prioritize his priorities. He said "prioritize priorities" out loud. It was not funny for the outside world, but it was for him. "Prioritize priorities" sounded like a speech exercise you'd do in a theatre class.

He wanted to walk on, but it was clear that he had not gone unnoticed. How could it be otherwise? The park was small, and they were the only two in each other's field of vision. It also felt like he was the first one who had shared this park with the woman in quite some time.

Normally, he would have walked on despite this insight. But it seemed too late. The woman looked pointedly in his direction, as though she'd recognized him and was trying to think who this man was again.

It was something he had almost gotten used to, though not quite. One of the smallest side effects of the acquisition was that he had become something of a celebrity. Not an A-lister. Rather, he was about as well-known as someone who'd had many supporting roles in various television series.

He was regularly featured in certain newspapers. Fortunately, the newspapers and magazines were read by businessmen and academics for the most part—not really the types who would want a selfie with him. But now and again, there'd be a student who, strangely enough, had become a kind of fanboy. The first time that had happened, everything was super awkward. He was new to the world of selfies, especially selfies of himself with others. A teenager, maybe just about to turn twenty, had walked up to him. What he remembered most of all was his huge backpack. He had never seen a backpack put to such an extreme test that it was bulging so much. It seemed to contain a good part of the books from the local library.

"Sir? Sir!"

It was only at the second "sir" that David knew the fanboy meant him.

"Can I have my photo taken with you?"

Who was he to say no? He did *want* to say no. He saw no benefit to himself in having his picture taken with this young man. But saying no would lead to a feeling of guilt that would be stronger than the discomfort he would feel as the picture was being taken.

"No problem," David said with a tone that would make most people realize that it actually *was* a problem.

David looked around to see whether there was anyone who could take the picture. But before he knew it, the boy threw an arm over his shoulders, as if they had known each other for years and were at a sing-along event together. That would have been the worst nightmare possible for David.

So there they stood, with the boy's arm slung over David's shoulders. The boy held out his arm and with one hand, clicked a number of photos on his phone, which was almost as big as a tablet.

Fortunately, he took several photos so that, by the last one, David had been able to force a smile. The boy had walked away happy, and David had felt used, a feeling compensated for in part by the boy's happy face.

Since then, it had happened more often, whether he was asked for a selfie or someone just took a shot of him as he was passing on the street. It was just as common a thing as people waiting at traffic lights or someone honking at another driver for no good reason.

But the girl on the bench, or rather the young woman, was not taking pictures, and it didn't look as if she was getting ready to either. She just looked at him, or at least in his direction. She didn't move—not even a wave. Nevertheless, David felt compelled to walk in her direction. It was as if his body was running in that direction while his brain was rapidly coming up with arguments for doing anything but that.

# 25. NATASHA

It had been a tough few years—physically, though also mentally. But Natasha knew she'd always kept up a certain level of good health.

She'd exercised enough, eaten well, and drank hardly at all. And she certainly hadn't taken any drugs. She'd been stressed—not just a bit, but a lot, and not just now and then, but several times a day. Actually, it was constant. Yet according to Google, she could still describe herself as healthy.

She pinched her forearm. *What a ridiculous thing to do*, she thought, even as she did it. As if pinching yourself made visions go away. Or was it that she would wake up from the pain and realize that the images were nothing but dreams, some kind of augmented reality?

She looked again. She was sure she was going off the deep end. This guy—in this place. It was easy to figure out; she didn't need to be some highly qualified psychotherapist. She'd been unhappy for years after he had sold what had been her higher calling. He'd become stinking rich, while she'd seen her higher calling turn into an utterly amorphous, faceless enterprise. Had she gone mad after all? Had what he'd done brought her to the point where her brain was tricking her with visions of him, the very source of all her current misery? Was this somehow going to help her cope?

She looked around. There was no other sign of life nearby. If she shouted something and it didn't mean anything, nobody would notice. So it was just something between her and the images in her head.

"Hello? Anybody there?"

The image of her old boss hadn't gone anywhere. Just as she'd done, he was now looking uneasily around him. There was a magnetic force drawing him toward her. She felt it, and he clearly did too. "He" was probably not him at all, but something conjured up by some algorithm in her brain.

Despite the magnetic force, the image was still standing there. His legs did not move, but it seemed the rest of his person was already coming toward her.

"David?"

She was shocked at herself. It was very amicable. They had worked together, at least in her mind. She had stood between the same four walls several times. There was even a handshake. (She would remember it well later.) But still, she would understand if he did not know her name, even if she'd probably hold that against him. Remembering even that basic fact was the least he could do after all she had done for him.

Her former boss's legs started carrying him toward her, slowly and clearly reluctantly. He was looking off to one side even as he approached.

What if this was not real, just a hallucination? How long would this game go on for? Had her body figured out how to help her process this? Or should she resist it? How much good could come from a conversation with a ghost— the ghost of a man who'd played a part in her life, even though she hadn't in his?

He was now quite close. The smell of the atmosphere was slowly changing. She could remember ghost stories where this change in smell would take place. It was starting to look more and more real, this ghost—or possibly this living man—saying nothing but standing quite close by, his hands in his pockets, his chin tucked under the upturned collar of his coat.

"Would you like to sit down?"

Natasha pointed to the spot to her left. That was a bit odd, since there would have been more room on the right.

At least half a minute followed.

Her old boss sat down. Or most likely the image of her old boss, as she kept telling herself.

His scent and his presence were starting to feel less and less ghostly. This hallucination had been made very credible by her brain.

Another long silence—this time a minute or more.

They both stared straight in front of them. Neither said anything. He seemed to be looking at the row of trees, which seemed to have been planted just to make this little square look more like a park. Natasha looked vaguely in the direction of the same white plastic bag. She thought it might have escaped by now, but its struggles were to no avail.

Her brain was going ninety to the dozen, trying to think of what she might say. It wasn't as though she was looking for an opening line, as if this were a first date. At the same time, she didn't want to blurt out any old thing that she might say to some stranger. And if this *was* David and not some apparition, she didn't want to be too friendly either. He had to know what he had done, what the consequences had been for people like her. But she didn't want to scare him away either. And besides, it was because of him that she had gained all that experience. Still, she refused to make him bigger than who he was to her. She was not about to treat him differently because of his fame and certainly not because of his outsized bank account.

She stood up. She surprised herself. David also looked up in surprise. She was just about to say something, but then she changed her mind. She looked around and again saw the plastic bag, still snagged on the branch of the log, which was heavier than she was.

"I—"

She hesitated. She had to seize the moment. Her words would have to come out. They'd have to make an impression on him and stick with him. She looked to one side again, removing the hair that had been blown into her face by the wind.

"How could you? How could you?" She'd been unleashed. "I gave you my all. Never nagged you about money, overtime, or promotions. I did everything in my power to make your dream come true. And I wasn't the only one. We believed in your vision. We were there for more than a career and a path to financial freedom. We all wanted to make your dream come true. We wanted to give everyone access to healthy food. I can still hear you say it!"

Now she had really hit her stride. This was something she had never done before. But halfway through her monologue, her arms started moving like the wings of a bird of prey that was about to strike.

"We were behind you. Whatever might've happened, we would build your dream. I was even prepared to work for months without a salary. If that isn't loyalty, I don't know *what* is! You can't ask for more than that. All those weekends, all those evenings when I could have been out meeting the man of my dreams. They were all for *your* dream, your vision."

She hadn't been prepared for the lump she now got in her throat. She wanted to be angry and make this meeting memorable with a show of anger. But her anger was now turning to sadness, or perhaps even some kind of desperation.

"Are you happy with all that money? Have you bought everything you wanted? Does it feel good to never have to do anything you don't want to do? Is it worth it? How do you feel about its being at the expense of people like me? You left us with nothing. No, that's not it. It's that you left our child with a different father, a father who milked it for all it was worth and PowerPointed the soul out of it. Was it worth it? Are you happy with your cars and your grand palace? Do you still think of us from your plane or when you're bragging to other captains of industry about your achievements? You should be ashamed of yourself, living your dreams at the expense of people like me. People who've given you their all. You got my best years. Hours that were mine actually weren't mine at all—they were yours. So how does that feel? How?"

Natasha interrupted her monologue. She looked to one side, not wanting to show him her face, even though she thought he should see it.

There was silence again. Natasha sat down on the bench again. This time, they used the space on the bench much more efficiently. She was waiting for a response from him, even though she was also satisfied with the icy silence.

# 26. BERNARD

"Bernard?"

"Mr. Chairman . . ."

"My sincere apologies, Mr. Chairman."

Bernard wanted to keep things formal wherever possible. He also liked a clear hierarchy so he felt he could keep control. He also now saw this project as more than just a project. It could become his life's work, his legacy. If he could manage the rejuvenation, he could extend the life of this institution by decades. If this succeeded—and he kept telling himself it would—everyone would remember only the chairman. Everyone has heard of Neil Armstrong, but who remembers Michael Collins?

The week before this first meeting, he had been busy working on the agenda. The presentation, in particular, was done to perfection. He'd had lengthy discussions with the printer about the weight of the paper and the font to be used for the hifalutin words.

In terms of content, the agenda for the evening was hardly original—why reinvent the wheel?—but the heavier paper and the italicized font gave the evening a certain gravitas. He also thought it was a weighty subject, and he had prepared just that answer in case someone asked about the reason for the heavy paper.

"Gentlemen, let us begin."

The table of old men cleared their throats and set down their drinks. Some put on their reading glasses. Others raised their hands to order another drink.

"Our mission is of vital importance. If we fail to rejuvenate this fine institution, it will perish with us."

Bernard was bothered by his treasurer. Instead of paying attention, he was more concerned about getting a new drink. He tried not to be visibly disturbed by it in front of the whole group, but he wanted to let him know with a stern face that this was not acceptable.

The nonverbal message came across, not only to the treasurer, but to the entire table. Everyone stopped doing whatever else they were doing out of fear—not of Bernard, but of how long this and subsequent meetings might last.

"As I said, we have the important task of saving this institution—of saving it by rejuvenating it and by selecting and creating a new crop of members to secure the decades ahead."

At least half a minute's silence followed. Bernard was keen to make sure that the weight and importance of the task at hand were clear to everyone. But the table seemed to be waiting for someone to break the silence.

At length, he obliged: "Let's get on with the agenda."

Everyone picked up the piece of paper that had been put on the table in front of them. Bernard had asked the staff to distribute them a few minutes before the start. Nobody said anything about the weight of the paper or the font.

The first item on the agenda was to write down the names of all attendees. That seemed to take forever. Bernard made sure that all titles were included and had each attendee spell out his full name. Unfortunately, a lot of the names included middle names and double-barreled surnames, so this ritual took an age to get through.

"Agenda item two."

Bernard looked around. The table seemed to be paying barely any attention by this point. On the one hand, this hurt him. Was he the only one who saw the importance of this mission? But he soon straightened his back and raised his chin. This was an opportunity. It would be even easier to get his way.

Bernard decided not to even read the agenda item. He went straight on the attack.

"An open evening. An evening with contemporary music, a menu that belongs to these times, and a speaker—a speaker who can capture the imagination and attract young people. The right young people, ambitious young men, coupled with a good check on their education, origins, and preferences."

The word "preferences" did not go down well. Some of the men shifted uncomfortably in their seats, and a few started talking in low tones, their heads lowered. That made Bernard uncomfortable. The cumulative age of those around the table might have been more than one thousand years, but no one was xeno- or homophobic.

"Excuse me. Naturally, what I meant was 'education and upbringing.'"

Education seemed a better word to Bernard. It was still a clear criterion by which they could separate the wheat from the chaff, but without all kinds of awkward political incorrectness.

"Our representative will be the most important ambassador. We will have to send him out to the right spots and make clear his association with us—universities, as well as multinationals and golf and tennis clubs where we can find a good number of young adults.

Things went quiet again. But a much less uncomfortable silence. People agreed with him. He was the leader he knew he could be.

"Our representative needs to have a reputation. This must be someone that everyone in our target group will recognize. Someone they look up to, someone they want to associate with. We will be like Nike shoes, worn by those who want to be associated with Michael Jordan."

Bernard was proud of his analogy—he thought it was slick and hip. He didn't know he'd mispronounced both "Nike" and even "Michael."

"Bernard? Sorry to interrupt, but what about your son?"

"I'm his father, and of course I have the greatest respect for him."

"As our representative?"

"Oh, I see. Yes, what a good idea."

The plan had succeeded. His surname would become the magnet for the young generation. With his son on that poster and then on the stage here at the club, it would be even clearer who had saved the institution.

"Are there any other suggestions?"

Bernard wanted to appear impartial, so he was willing to take this risk because half the table was busy with their new drink or calling again for another round.

"No one?"

In the corner of his eye, he saw someone getting ready to make a suggestion. Bernard spoke before they could get a word out.

"Good, if this is what you wish. I will, of course, take the lead on this, and my son will be there for us. Does anyone have preferences regarding music or other entertainment for our young audience? How about we have someone take charge of public relations and the distribution of communications?"

The table was silent. The gentlemen had clearly joined the committee as an excuse to come to the club. It seemed as if no one was willing to do anything other than that.

"How about we outsource it? I can arrange something through the universities. I didn't lend my name to these institutions for years for nothing."

Bernard thought it was a good idea. But this would only be for distribution. He had to, and would, control the form and the way communications were generated.

"That's a great idea. If you want to prepare the distribution network, that would be great. Given all your busy schedules, I will take care of the printing."

Bernard had now learned that it was fool-proof to emphasize how busy everyone was. All members of the club insisted they were still really busy. Bernard had heard from some that they were even busier after retirement than before. He did not want to go that far, but he understood that it was necessary to keep his diary full, or at least to convey the impression that it was.

What the committee did not know was that Bernard already had a first version of the poster at home. He had used a photo of his son with himself subtly but visibly behind him. He had also made his surname bigger than the rest of the text. Of course, his son's first name was in front of it, but he had given it a much less prominent place.

He knew that his son could tell his story in his sleep. He had heard him speak on different media platforms before. He did not want to scare his son—he had already spoken once at the club. Bernard understood that if he asked David again, he might put him off.

The invitation should seem as though it was for some festive gathering. He envisioned an inaugural dinner, a gathering of like-minded souls. David would surely think that was worthwhile. And then, just after the soup had been served, he would ask him to tell his story one more time. Unbeknownst to him, that would be the reason all the younger guests had come. Peer pressure would easily get his son on stage.

"Gentlemen, there are other agenda items. However, given the last constructive minutes, I think they will be unnecessary. Besides, you are busy enough already. Let's embark on the course of action we've been discussing. It will be quite something."

The men raised their glasses, relieved that they did not have to finish the rest of the agenda—and all the more so since they didn't have to do anything, just be there and spell out their names, including titles.

# 27. DAVID

He could not yet decide what he was more ashamed of, or rather, what he felt more guilty about. Was it everything that this woman thought he was guilty of, or was it the fact that he could not really remember her?

Apparently, she had done a lot for him for a long time. For him! And yes, she was not satisfied with the acquisition, but then again, neither was he. Worse yet, though, this unknown woman had lived in his circle for a long time—for years—but he could not remember her.

David wanted to treat her as a human being, as a former colleague. But he realized that there was more going on here. He'd heard most of what she'd said, but he was mostly occupied with his own thoughts and studying this stranger. When he was a teenager, his male friends had always talked about "hot girls," making all kinds of swirling and thrusting movements with their hips. That was not his thing. He would often laugh along out of politeness, and so they wouldn't know that he was even more of an outsider than they already thought he was.

But there was something about the way she looked: her jawline, her neck. The hair that she clumsily had to remove from her left eye. She was beautiful. But he was not allowed to be having these thoughts. He had to listen to the content: her anger and her unhappiness, which were of his making. The least he could do was listen and, with a bit of luck, come up with an answer or some sort of explanation.

She went on for a while—it was a monologue full of passion. Her arms suggested that she was going to go on the attack one way or another. There was a clear theme in her speech. Something she kept repeating in various phrases. She had given him more than, strictly speaking, had been agreed upon. He had come out ahead. She hadn't.

He caught himself wanting to put himself in a victim's position at first. Yes, he had sold the company. But he had never regretted anything more than he regretted that—especially knowing what he knew now. He should have thought like Mark Zuckerberg—withstand all the giant bids and build RoboWok into a world power himself. They were already farther along than Facebook was then, and they were already much harder to catch up with. If he had known what life would be like after the acquisition, he would never have done it. Such emptiness. Such an aimless existence.

Still, taking this position would have been quite out of place. He was not happy, but what he saw before him seemed to be in a different league of misery altogether. How could such a beautiful creature be so unhappy? In the normal course of things, he might have walked away or given a very brief matter-of-fact reply in the middle of someone else's speech. But this was different. There was the fact that he had come here without a plan. Even cycling, the only plan there'd been, had failed. And now, here in this little park, possibly the smallest park in the Northern Hemisphere, he meets this very woman.

She'd stopped. She was sitting next to him, looking straight ahead. She had a hollow, empty look in her eyes, not unlike the one he oftenhad in his since he'd lost RoboWok.

The silence was uncomfortable. She was clearly waiting for a response. David wanted to say something, but he had calculated that the utility of a quick response did not outweigh that of a better one, even if the latter took longer.

It went against everything he usually applied to life, to his work. Normally, he would have quickly assessed the situation, formed a hypothesis about the right course of action, and then done a quick sanity check. The incremental value of each second was therefore low, with even less value for each second that followed.

But this was different. He imagined possible responses, weighed them up, and thought of subsequent responses based on possible scenarios. The stakes were quite high. There was his self-image, her happiness, and perhaps, if he came up with a good enough response, the chance to see her again.

Minutes passed. She did not speak, and it was clear that she was going to wait for his response, however long it took in coming. She had spoken. She'd said a lot, and it had taken her quite some time. It was apparently enough for her.

David put out his right hand, palm upward, as though he were about to deliver a heartfelt speech. But his mouth didn't open, and he let his hand fall again. Back to the drawing board.

She had looked up expectantly but soon realized that she would have to wait a little longer.

Things were getting evermore awkward by the minute. David felt the pressure building. He couldn't just say nothing. The longer he took to start talking, the more pressure he felt to say something that would be all-encompassing and solve everything.

He had never thought about the art of speechwriting—about the men and women who write what presidents and CEOs tell their audiences. Pieces of text where every word is weighed and measured by armies of media professionals, potential voters, employees, or shareholders. It was an art that he'd never mastered—far from it. He always liked to keep things short and well-structured. Situation. Complication. Resolution. He wanted the people who heard him to focus on deeds, not words.

He sighed.

"You're right."

It was not exactly "I Have a Dream" or "Ich bin ein Berliner." But David was not entirely dissatisfied with his first three words. They were for her, and he was speaking the truth for the most part—something he'd always found to be a good strategy.

"For what you've done for me, I can never repay you. And for what it's worth, I agree with you completely. I should never have sold it. Yes,

I have bought all kinds of things. I reluctantly thought of things to buy. Was it worth it? No. Could I have thought of this beforehand? Perhaps. It felt like a triumph, turning my idea and our work into such a huge amount of money. Throughout your life, you hear that money is the goal and that it's going to solve everything. In the papers and on TV, you see all kinds of happy people in their Lamborghinis with their designer sunglasses. And the people with their yachts in Monaco seem even happier. You're right—you're absolutely right. Having money is convenient, but from a certain point on, every extra cent is completely unnecessary. You replace things you already have with something bigger and shinier. You eat things that are hard to come by and not necessarily tasty. And you create living spaces that you hardly ever see. Would I have done things differently with these insights? Well, of course. I made that mistake. I created my own problem. But now that I hear that people like you have also become unhappy because of it, it hurts me. I hear you. Really, I have no words to express how grateful I am to you. You had a contract, and we both had rights. But what you have done goes well beyond that. It's unique. And that this should happen to me is really beyond belief. I can't say how grateful I am to you."

There was silence again. David was hoping for a response. He was not dissatisfied with the one he had just given. Looking back, he could have said certain things differently, but this was all right. He thought he was right, again. All those minutes spent thinking were unnecessary. What he had said had already occurred to him in the first minute. Any extra second, any extra minute would hardly have made it better.

There they sat, in silence. He was still waiting for her to speak. She was waiting for a further response from him. Or did they both want what they now had—the silence? That was unclear, and for the time being, no one wanted to take the initiative.

Fifteen minutes or more had passed. Something changed in David's mind. Enough gloom, enough looking back on mistakes—something had to be done.

"We have to keep going."

She looked up, puzzled.

"We can sit here for hours, thinking and talking about my mistakes and the consequences for both of us. You know what will come of that? Zilch. Nada. We have to do something about it."

David had deliberately said "us." He felt he had to solve this for both of them—or at least for her.

"I will buy you anything you want, although I don't think an object is going to be the solution. But it's your choice, even if it is a house or an investment in the business you have always wanted to start. Just say the word. Or words— however many you need."

David expected a different look from what he saw. There was less emptiness in her gaze, but that was all.

"I see. You are farther along than I was when I sold. You understand that having stuff is not what any of this is about."

She looked straight in front of her, motionless. She didn't have to move. This was the most convincing way of endorsing what he had said.

"And you shouldn't make any decisions now. Me neither. There's a solution. There always is. Instead of thinking of all the consequences, we should focus on the very next step. If that turns out to be in the wrong direction, then we'll think of something else. I will not be a genie who pops out of a bottle and gives you only one wish."

He actually saw a bit of life in her face—the faintest of smiles.

"What can you do tomorrow that will make that day better than today? It doesn't have to be anything big. I'm open to anything, to be honest. It's not my thing, but if it's buying clothes or going to some magic show, just say it. It's whatever you want. Just say the word."

He himself felt increasing energy. Solving this problem was stirring something within him. It was as if a project had come his way, something with some meaning. It might not be a new company, a new purchase, or a new building project. It was smaller, or perhaps bigger just for that reason. How could he improve the life of this stranger?

"Seriously. Don't try to come up with something big. Nothing will solve everything at once. Nothing can make up for what I did—all those days it cost you. Start with something to do. Don't think about why it can't be done. Time and money—that's my problem. Tomorrow, or even now, we can take the first step. Whatever you want. Was it a good first step? Good! Then we take the next one. Was it a bad one? No problem. We'll just give something else a go.

David wanted to tackle it just as he had tackled his business ideas—always focusing on the next step. Don't do anything stupid, but don't dwell too long on all the choices you have before you either. Trust that a first hypothesis, with a few iterations, can move things in the right direction. Chances are that it's the best idea out there—certainly if you stack it up against the cost of weeks spent thinking.

Still no response from her. But something had changed. His words were having an effect. She didn't laugh, but she didn't look unhappy either. She put both hands under her thighs and started swinging her feet back and forth. She was working on something.

"Tell me. What are you thinking? Can we take a first step? Really, no idea is too ridiculous. And nothing is final. I'm keen to think along with you. Do you want a house? Then we'll make an appointment with a real estate agent right now. Whatever you want."

She reached into her coat pocket and took out her phone, which was in a case with a leopard-skin pattern. It was charming. It made him even more eager to help her—or actually, himself.

He tried to guess what she was looking up on her phone. He couldn't look. He made a point of looking away. Was she looking for houses? Was she going to show him an empty storefront? She didn't seem the type for that. Maybe she was looking for a puppy or a musical instrument. That seemed to suit her better.

She was busy, clearly not going back to a page on the internet that she had had open for months. It seemed like she was putting something together. And, in fact, that is just what she was doing: putting something together, and then doing that again, and then yet again. Was it a car after all? Or a custom-built house with all kinds of overvalued options? Had he misjudged her? Was this going to be old-fashioned materialism after all? He hoped not. He was hoping that there was something more than a transaction in the offing. Most of all, he was hoping he could help her and, in the process, see her more often.

He felt the phone in his side. She was prodding him—letting him look at her phone. He closed his eyes for a moment, all but praying to a god he didn't believe in that it would be something meaningful.

He picked up the phone. It was blocked. She soon realized and reopened the screen with a four-digit combination. He didn't want to see it, but he knew it had to be her birthday.

He looked at the screen; the thing he saw was a sum of money. Five digits. He was hopeful. It could be a car. That was the worst-case scenario. But given the user interface on the web page, this seemed most unlikely.

He scrolled down with his right index finger. He saw a whole list of airports, dates.

A trip around the world. She'd chosen an experience, not a thing.

The strange woman, or the strange girl, turned out to be even more beautiful and better than he might have wished for. What a good first choice. Not possessions but experiences. She was wise. She got it.

"This is a perfect first step! It will not solve everything, but at least it is an experience. A lot of experiences. Use that time, even if you find yourself on a tropical island thinking that you wanted a house after all!"

David looked through the journey again. It was very detailed. The route, the schedule. She'd been thinking about this for quite some time. It was perfect—and the perfect start to his project.

"One question."

She looked up, and her smile quickly gave way to a look of doubt. She seemed to be disappointed already. She had clearly been disappointed many times in her life and now expected to be disappointed yet again—this time by him.

"Why would you fly economy?"

# 28. BERNARD AND DAVID

avid picked up the phone.

"My son."

"Father."

"Well, that could be a bit more cheerful, don't you think? Your father has come to you with some fabulous news!"

David thought that as sure as eggs is eggs, how fabulous the news was depended on who was hearing it. He was certain he would be quite underwhelmed by it. Still, he wanted to keep things nice and pleasant. Who was he to burst his father's happy bubble?

"Oh, do tell." He was doing a terrible job of faking curiosity, but his father seemed not to notice and was enthused.

"The adjudication committee has taken another look at your profile, and the good news is that you've passed with flying colors. Of course, how could it have been otherwise, given our bloodline?"

"Yes—three cheers for our Grade A Certified DNA. Bully for us."

Remarkably, Bernard did not notice the sarcasm.

"Fantastic, right? And to give the news a festive angle, in exactly two weeks' time, there will be an opening dinner, and we'll all be there."

"All?"

"Anyone who's anyone among the members, my lad. This is something quite unique. Normally, the first thing you do is spend many months trying to get in, writing letter after begging letter. And then, even once you *are* in, you're lucky if you can get a spot anywhere near the bar or the stage. But you, my lad—you might even get to be *on* the stage!"

"On the *stage*?" This was becoming a bit much. He was fine with the membership—it was clear it meant a lot to his father. It was a small gesture, and it was nothing compared to raising the little boy that David once was. It was the least he could do. But standing onstage again?

"Father, I've already spoken, right?"

"Yes, you're right, my lad. Forget it. Just come and have a bite—on the house. We'll talk about this and that, just shoot the breeze, and perhaps there's something you might also like to talk about. We'll see on the night."

Bernard felt sure that, once there, his son wouldn't be able to resist the peer pressure. All he would have to do was let him into the building, and the rest would follow.

Father, I'm honored—I really am—and I would consider membership an honor. But being as active as you are there is not yet a real option for me. Perhaps later."

"I understand, my lad. I do. As I said, just come along. You'll have to eat something anyway, won't you?"

"True."

Even as he answered, though, David felt in his gut what his father's thinly veiled agenda was. The details were not that clear, but what *was* clear was that he was being used either to fill up another evening or as a magnet for much younger men interested in his story.

It was quiet for a moment—uncomfortably so. David quickly tapped his wooden desk with the nail of his left index finger, hoping somehow that the panicky tap-tap-tap would dissipate the awkwardness of the silence.

Luckily, Bernard broke the silence. "My son, your father would be only too delighted if you would come along. If need be, we can grab a bite together in a quiet corner—father-son time, nothing more."

David wasn't falling for it. That much was clear. Yet the tone in his father's voice was unmistakable. He needed this. He was desperate for his son's time. David felt he could not abandon him. And still, he could not let himself be used like that. Was this a father's love for his son? Would this have happened if he had not made something of his life?

And all his choices, all his steps toward RoboWok, had been in spite of what his father had wanted. Bernard had had a completely different path in mind for him—one strewn with titles and a CV filled with the names of big players.

He had to be above this—though, now that he thought about it, what did "above this" actually mean? Leaving his father in the lurch and hurting his feelings? Or should he just get it over with? How many lessons could he still teach his father, who wasn't, after all, getting any younger? He had been molded into the man he was a long time ago. Could he still be changed?

Could he help it that he'd grown up in a class society where your CV gave you not just bragging rights but also a much better chance of survival? It was the best thing a father could do for his son, at least in his mind.

"So then, my boy, can I count on you?"

"Father." David wanted to be a man of his word. This was the moment to bite the bullet, either with a message of obedience or by saying that this was going too far.

"It would make your father proud as a peacock."

His father sounded fragile. David was not used to this desperation. However, it was still theatricality of the first walk. This whole business had nothing to do with David and everything to do with his father, who would actually be proud as a peacock of himself, of his genes, of his "parenting methods."

Some childhood memories flashed through David's mind. If his father were to publish his "parenting methods," it would be the skimpiest of pamphlets—no doubt with a nice cover featuring some clever catch phrases and barely a scrap inside.

"What time does it start at?"

"The drinks start at five o'clock, as always."

"No. I mean, what time do you really want me there?"

"What are you saying, my lad?"

"I don't need a drink. And there'll be a good chance, in fact, that I'll already have had something to eat. But I'll be there when you need me. So exactly what time do I need to be there at?"

David could hear his father busy with papers at the other end of the line. It took a while—and it also seemed as if his father had dropped something heavy. That made his search longer.

"Once again, my son, it would be nice if you could join us for dinner. That way you can get to know the society and its members. There are many really inspiring men among them. Perhaps I know someone who can help you with your taxes."

"Father, I will be there. But only for what I'm needed for. Just let me know right when I need to be there so I can do my thing and then leave your club without anyone's noticing."

"Club? Society, my lad—and it's your society too."

"Society, then. My apologies, father."

"If you are there at five minutes before nine o'clock, I will make sure everyone is ready for you."

David's strict and businesslike tone and approach had worked. Bernard was clear this time that he was expecting his son to perform— to stand onstage, tell his story, and make it clear that he shared a surname with the organizer of the evening. It was not about him, or even his story. It was a party trick he'd be doing—putting on an exhibition of his father's certified Grade A genetics.

"Will you send someone to pick me up? I would like to walk from the front door directly to the stage."

"If that is what you want, fine. Again, you are welcome to come earlier and certainly to leave later. Food and drinks are on the house, my lad, so enjoy them on us."

"I'll send you the address later. The driver can pick me up there. And could you make sure it's a nice car?"

"You're not coming from home?"

"I don't think so. I'll send it to you as soon as I can. Again, let's not waste time. As soon as the driver drops me off, I want to go from the front door to the stage." This time, David himself was shocked by how stern his tone was.

"As you wish, my lad. Again, let's make a nice evening of it. So many like-minded souls, so many nice things to enjoy together."

"I'll send the address to you as soon as possible, father."

# 29. MARIA

Maria hardly ever got a good night's sleep. Sleeping either not properly or not at all had become the rule.

She'd tried everything. A week before, she'd removed every clock, charger—anything that gave off the slightest buzz, click, or hum that even a dog wouldn't hear. She had to do everything she could to get these few hours of sleep. Her body was always jaded. But the problem was what was going on in her head. No matter what she tried, her brain kept churning out the most frightful scenarios, replaying all the wrong decisions and, in particular, speculating about the consequences that could have befallen her.

Usually, after repeated attempts, she managed to rack up a few hours' worth of sleep, but the night before, she hadn't managed to get even a wink.

She'd been awake for so long that her body no longer wanted to lie down. She'd started trudging around, as slowly and lackadaisically as it was possible to go without actually coming to a standstill. She had warmed up some milk— a few glasses' worth. She'd been convinced that glasses one and two would help her sleep, but she'd drank glass three pretty much so as not to waste milk.

Now it was evening, and her son was in bed. She could try again. Her body was, as always, weary, but this time her thoughts seemed to cooperate as well. The only thing she could think of was sleeping. Even brushing her teeth was a major effort. In the end, she'd given them just a quick brush. She associated the taste of toothpaste with going to bed, so just five seconds of brushing did the trick.

She undressed with some difficulty and threw herself onto her smaller part of the bed. The pillow under her head felt simply divine. Her toes touched the inside of her duvet.

She needed this. At least this was a form of happiness.

"Maria?"

Maria didn't hear. She was out like a log. It would've taken a take a brass band to wake her.

"Maria. Maria-a-a-a!"

That did the trick, or just about. She opened her eyes and sat up, even if she was still not fully alert.

Maria felt a hand on her shoulder. A touch that felt like it came from a stranger rather than from her husband. There'd been no physical contact between her and her husband for years.

"Come, come. There's a man at the door. He's wearing a hat."

The word "hat" seemed to work wonders.

"A hat? A man with a hat?"

In a matter of seconds, Maria went from barely awake to DEFCON 1.

"The police! Is it the police?"

Maria panicked. She looked around for something to put on. She threw on her first choice, an old T-shirt. She realized she might have to keep wearing for a while whatever she put on.

She then put on her husband's track suit, which was way too big for her, and headed to the door, putting her hair into a tight ponytail as she went. In the back of her mind, she had the idea that pulling her hair tight would give her the best-groomed look, perhaps even making the case for her innocence.

She put her hand on the doorknob and took two deep, quiet breaths. It was something she had practiced a lot during the last year. She'd become a past master at suffering in silence.

She pulled the door open and felt a wave of relief come over her.

"You're not from the police?"

"Police? Ha ha. Not me, ma'am. Do you see a mustache?"

Maria didn't get the thing about the moustache. Did cops have to have a moustache in this country?

"What can I help you with?" It was a phrase she used often, and it usually put stressed-out people that were asking a lot quickly at ease.

"I've come to collect you, ma'am."

"'Ma'am'? I'm not usually called that."

The unknown man in the hat did not react. In fact, his expression didn't change at all. Maria decided to enjoy this rather formal way of talking.

"Are you sure you're in the right place? Where are you taking me?"

"Are you Maria?"

"Yes—though that's not the most unique name in the world. Just saying."

"Yes, I'm in the right place, ma'am. I've been in the business for over thirty years. I don't make mistakes like that."

"Oh, I'm sure. But please do tell me where you're planning on taking me. Who do you work for?"

"The society, ma'am. I was sent to pick you up, with clear instructions. We need to hurry. This detour means we're behind schedule."

Maria went right back into a panic, though she tried not to let it show. This could mean only one thing. He'd found out. She knew it—she'd been caught.

Maria tried to remain calm, but she couldn't stop the tears from welling up.

"Do I have time to change?"

"No, ma'am. You have to come with me now. I have never been late, and I'm not about to start now."

There was no negotiating with this guy. Maria knew that she would have to go with him. She could probably postpone her fate, but a man of his means would surely have a cohort of men with hats at his disposal who could pick her up wherever she went. She did not want to live as a refugee. She had just come here with the promise of more freedom.

"Can I at least get my coat?"

Without being asked, the man in the hat took a coat for her off one of the hooks just inside the door. And in fact, it was the one she would've picked. It wasn't that clever of him, though—she was the only woman in the house, and there weren't that many coats.

Maria put on the coat and walked out, head bowed, behind the stranger. She tried to make peace with her fate. Perhaps now she would at least be able to go back to sleep with a clearer conscience.

From the stairwell, she quickly called out instructions to her husband. Her son would have to go to school the next day, even if she wasn't there. Her husband did not respond.

Downstairs, she saw a huge car in front of her. The wheels in particular stood out. They seemed to be as big as those on a bus.

"Now I know for sure that you're not from the police."

"What do you mean, ma'am?"

"The police would never be allowed to drive an American luxury car like this." Maria meant it as a joke, just to break the ice.

"It's a German car, ma'am—a Maybach. Originally made by the company that made Zeppelins."

"But it doesn't fly, I guess."

"No, ma'am. It doesn't fly."

Once again, the expression of the man in the hat, who turned out to be a chauffeur, remained unchanged.

The back seat felt bigger than her sofa. She looked at the back of the driver's seat. It had a built-in TV screen showing all kinds of information. There was nothing about where she was being taken, though plenty about the weather and her current address, which she already knew.

"There's chilled water in the armrest next to you, if you like."

Maria looked to one side and pulled out a leather tab. Behind the leather armrest there was indeed a chilled bottle of water with two crystal glasses in front of it. It made no impression. Maria thought mostly about how over the top this all was.

She did feel that she could use a glass of water, though. She did her best to get the water from the bottle into one of the glasses in the already moving car. It worked, but barely.

It didn't matter to her where she was going. That wasn't what was important. She hoped above all that it would not be too painful. She was ready to accept being fired in the normal way. She accepted her fate and hoped above all that the damage would be limited.

Then she began to fret. Her head began once again to run unbidden through all kinds of horrible scenarios. She tried to stop it but to no avail. She wanted to enjoy this nice drive—the moments before the misery would begin. Tomorrow she would have to deal with the consequences. For the moment, she preferred to stay ignorant.

She looked out the window. They had clearly been on the road longer than she'd realized. The shop fronts were quite different.

There were Italian and French names in gold and white reflecting letters.

The car stopped. Would she be meeting her boss here? Was his idea to get in a bit of shopping while accepting her resignation? She couldn't decide what was going on. On the one hand, she felt pretty good because he would think it was a no-brainer and could take things in his stride. On the other, she was hoping for a bit of drama. Maybe it would make her feel like she was a Real Somebody.

The door of the German car opened, and she was met by the same feelingless gaze.

"Come with me, ma'am."

Maria took a deep breath and started clambering out of the deep bucket seat. The driver extended a hand—another luxury, though not unnecessary in this case.

No sooner was she standing straight than an overly made-up woman approached her.

"Welcome, welcome. Just lovely. We can certainly make something beautiful out of this."

Uninvited, the woman began to touch Maria's hair. Not much later, Maria felt one of the woman's hands on her waist.

"Lovely proportions—really nice."

Maria was getting a lot of compliments, but the bizarreness of the situation stopped her from enjoying them. The man in the hat calling her ma'am, then the big German car, and now this. It was the opposite of what she'd been expecting.

A few minutes later, a second woman joined them. Together, they put up her hair, but they mainly talked about the possibilities associated with her, without even once asking her opinion.

A third woman came in to do her makeup. This was getting more bizarre by the minute.

In the meantime, a fourth person, this time a man, had started holding long dresses in front of her. They looked like gala dresses—she knew that from TV. They were worn by film stars, politicians, and CEOs.

Nobody asked her anything. Before she knew it, the man in the hat was helping her back into the German car. She saw herself in a mirror that was too small, in the front of a car that was too big. She had never looked like this in her entire life. She had made herself up before, and on her wedding day, she'd also worn a beautiful dress. But this was different— not necessarily prettier, but clearly a lot of time had been put into it by people who had done it before.

The dress prevented her from sitting down comfortably. That just added to the general discomfort of the whole situation.

Was she supposed to accept all this? Was it some kind of kindness? It was beginning to look more and more like a cruel joke. Pampering her right up until she was fired and thrown into handcuffs. Maybe she was going to be blackmailed. She had heard stories of rich men who considered themselves above everything else and found it normal to use women like her for all sorts of inhuman games. It began to look more and more like this was what was going on. Maria was suddenly seized by panic.

"Let me out!"

She tried to open the door of the car even as it was moving.

"Ma'am? Ma'am!"

The chauffeur turned on the child lock. That only made Maria panic even more. She tried to grab the driver from behind.

"Let me out! This has to stop!"

With some difficulty, and this time with something like emotion on his face, the driver pulled the car over to the side of the road.

He got out of Maria's rather weak grip.

"Calm down, ma'am. Calm down."

"What are you going to do with me! I don't deserve this. I'm a human being—a hardworking person!"

"Ma'am, please. We're almost there."

Maria hit her head on one of the screens on the back of the front seats. The knock calmed her down. It was as if she was at peace with her destiny again. This was the way things had to be.

The car came to a stop. The driver handed over a mirror.

"You may want to touch up your face again, ma'am."

Maria looked in the mirror. All the grimacing the panic had brought on had smudged her eyeliner. She tried to fix it.

The car door opened. The now-familiar hand came to help her clamber out again.

"Ma'am?"

"Here we go," Maria said to herself.

She followed the driver.

They went into an old building that had a lot of cars like the Maybach in front of it. Almost all of them were German, she now realized.

She saw an old wooden sign with the word "Society" on it. A word she vaguely knew but could not yet place.

Inside, her coat was taken.

She was led to a side door.

The situation was even more awkward, although Maria was, strangely, more compliant than ever. It seemed that she had gotten used to the bizarreness of the situation. She was facing her destiny. She would make the best of it, whatever it turned out to be.

She was led up a flight of stairs to a dark place next to a red curtain. She smelled the scent of cigars and heard a large group of men chattering away. They were deeper voices, presumably all belonging to men of a certain age.

A young boy dressed in a dinner jacket gave Maria a glass of water.

The boy wished her well.

She felt the panic slowly rising up in her again. It seemed darker than before. Her hands were shaking so much it was hard for her to drink.

She heard the boy say, "Listen. They're announcing you."

From behind the curtain, she heard an elderly man speaking through a microphone.

"Ladies and gentlemen, you've all been waiting months for this. The time has finally come. Today is the start of the next century of our club. Today, the rejuvenation begins. Without further ado, I will not keep you in suspense, it is my honor to introduce to you the newest and youngest member, my s—"

Before she could do anything about it, Maria had been ushered gently onto the stage.

# 30. NATASHA

Natasha was startled awake. She had a moment of panic because she'd forgotten that she'd fallen asleep with a cloth mask over her eyes.

There was a knock at the door. "Ma'am? Ma'am?" The accent was unfamiliar.

It took her a while, but then a bit of turbulence reminded her that she was several miles up. It wasn't her first time on a plane, but she had never woken up in a bed on a plane before. And not just any bed, but a double bed in a separate bedroom.

"Yes? Please come in."

The person behind the door, presumably a stewardess, did not enter. That was probably protocol.

"There is someone here to see you."

Now Natasha was really awake. She got up and opened the door to her "living room." She had stayed awake as long as she could. A living room and a bedroom in a plane, and everything she wanted could be ordered at the touch of a button. Against her better judgment, she had watched film after film, each time with another glass of champagne and one more slice of chocolate cake.

She quickly put on her dressing gown, which she was told she could keep. She had thought about this. She couldn't imagine that anyone who'd be in a cabin like this would have any wish to keep the airline's dressing gown.

"He can come in."

She quickly tried to do something with her hair. Makeup was no longer an option.

"Ma'am, your guest."

A living room and separate bedroom several miles up were a bizarre luxury, but Natasha still had to step aside to let her guest in.

"Good morning. May I come in?"

"But of course. You can take a seat in my living room." Natasha could've said this a thousand times over. She knew that there was a good chance she'd never have the occasion to again.

"Ha ha. Glad you're enjoying it."

"But of course. How could you possibly not enjoy this? If I had known you were coming, I would have set an alarm and cleaned up." Natasha looked around. To her surprise, everything had been completely tidied up for her while she'd been sleeping. It looked like the next passenger could already come in.

"Would you like some coffee? Or perhaps something else? We'll be landing shortly, so this is your last chance."

The flight attendant heard this and was back in an instant with breakfast menus. Natasha rattled off a long list of things she wanted for breakfast, and then asked, "Don't you want something?"

"A coffee, please. Black, no sugar."

"Don't you ever have breakfast?"

"I had breakfast over an hour ago. Since then, I've been begging the cabin staff to let me stop by here." He smiled at the stewardess.

"I thought all these suites were in the same part of the plane?"

"They are."

David smiled, knowing it would take time for Natasha to realize he was "merely" sitting in business class.

After a moment, the penny dropped. She stared at him, her mouth agape for a moment. "Then we'll swap places right this minute. I've had this part all to myself." Natasha hurriedly started to pack her things.

"No, no, sit down. Enjoy your breakfast. I'm doing just fine. Yesterday I had a meal, watched two films, and slept for six hours, pretty much soundly."

"But not in a bedroom."

"No—that's true."

"I am extremely grateful that you have given me this, but, don't get me wrong, you can easily book two suites like this, can't you?"

"Yes, I can."

"But you're saving up for another holiday?" Natasha thought this was hilarious, but she got just a small, though very sweet, smile in return.

"I'm not going to bore you with my thoughts on this for too long. Just enjoy it while you can."

"Oh no, you're going to sell me. That's human trafficking, you know." She shocked herself with her morbid sense of humor.

"I've flown in a suite like this several times. The first few times I slept for just a few hours— just like you, I imagine."

Natasha nodded and laughed.

"After the umpteenth time, the novelty wore off, and I was often preoccupied with the destination and with everything that was wait- ing for me there. And then I found out that, as with so much in life, 99 percent of the value lies in the journey, in simply being brought from A to B."

"But what else do you do with all that money? It gets you privacy, a better night's sleep, and so on."

"I still fly business class, even though I think it's also overpriced. That said, check-in is fast, and you can be among the first to leave the plane. You often get the same meal, only with fewer choices, which I don't want to make anyway. And sleeping in a plane is mostly an illusion. The TV screens are more than big enough, and at least no one bothers you while you're watching a movie."

"I guess you can see it that way."

"But this is not the point. It's not about me. Just enjoy it while you can."

"Again, a bit dramatic: 'while you can'!"

"You're right, it's a luxury problem. This is a luxury problem—knowing and often having experienced that from a certain point onwards, any incremental increase in luxury is extremely expensive but usually adds no value. The novelty is the saving grace in the short term, but when the sheen wears off, there's not that much left."

"Oh, wow! I was not expecting to feel this depressed from this conversation."

"I'm really going to stop now. Once again, enjoy it while it's still got this luster. Live in this moment, while it's still got some value. And by the way, you don't just have a living room and a bedroom—there's also a bathroom.

"Also overrated?"

"OK, maybe not that."

Natasha laughed and noticed that she kept looking at her traveling companion a little longer than was strictly necessary. And he also seemed to keep looking back just as long.

"Then I will take a nice long shower and have breakfast at the same time, challenging as that sounds."

"Enjoy. I'm going back to simply existing."

"In business class?"

They both laughed. He made to head off.

"David?"

Natasha took a step out of her suite. The staff looked at her as if this had never happened before.

"David?"

He turned around.

"When we arrive, what have you actually got going on?"

"Good question. I booked a hotel for my visa application, but that's purely because I needed an address."

"You have no plans?"

"I've booked a return trip for myself."

"Can you miss your flight back?"

* 9 7 8 1 9 6 4 9 3 4 1 1 2 *